Change of a Dress

Read all the Cinderella Cleaners books!

Change of a Dress

Prep Cool

MAYA GOLD

SCHOLASTIC INC.

New York   Toronto   London   Auckland
Sydney   Mexico City   New Delhi   Hong Kong

No part of this publication may be reproduced, stored in a retrieval system, or transmitted in any form or by any means, electronic, mechanical, photocopying, recording, or otherwise, without written permission of the publisher. For information regarding permission, write to Scholastic Inc., Attention: Permissions Department, 557 Broadway, New York, NY 10012.

ISBN-13: 978-0-545-12959-6
ISBN-10: 0-545-12959-1

12 11 10 9 8 7 6 5 4 3   10 11 12 13 14 15/0

Printed in the U.S.A.
First edition, April 2010

Book design by Yaffa Jaskoll

To the Rondout Drama Club posse

Chapter One

I'm in love with this view. It's the one truly fabulous thing about growing up in Weehawken, New Jersey: Every time I look east, even if it's just to gaze out the window during eighth-period math, my horizon is filled with the glittering skyline of midtown Manhattan.

Too bad there's a river between me and it.

My eyes follow a red tugboat pulling a barge about six times its size past the Statue of Liberty. There are cruise ships steaming away from the docks, headed for Cancun or Paradise Island, and planes angling upward from Newark Airport, sun glinting off silvery wings. Wherever I look, someone's leaving. Except me.

"Diana Donato?"

My math teacher, Mr. Perotta, has X-ray eyes. He can be drawing a graph on the board with his back to the room and still know who's paying attention and who's got one eye on the clock, or the school buses lining up outside the doors, or the Empire State Building. How does he do it? It must be some trick teachers practice at home.

I don't have a clue what question he's asked me. I hesitate, torn between telling the truth and making a wild flying guess, when the bell fills the air with the sound of freedom.

All around me, kids jump to their feet, scraping chairs and slamming books shut, and Mr. Perotta is so busy yelling, "Work sheets tomorrow! Graphs fifteen to twenty!" that I never have to confess my attention was miles away. *Whew!*

My best friend, Jessica Munson, comes up to me, digging an elbow into my side as we go into the hall. "Should I say it?"

"What?" asks our friend Sara Parvati, her ears always sharp.

"Saved by the bell," Jess intones with high drama. She tosses her head. I've always envied her wavy red hair — mine is boring dark brown — but she envies me being almost five feet six, so I guess we're even.

Sara groans and takes off with her soccer buddy, Amelia Williams, their ponytails bouncing in rhythm, one black and one blond. Jess shrugs and grins. "Well, I *asked*."

"No, you should not say it," I laugh. *"Rewind."*

I mime pushing the button on an imaginary remote and Jess takes a step backward, pretending to stuff the words back in her mouth. This is one of our bits. Sometimes we put each other into Fast Forward or Pause.

I'd like to put my whole life on Pause today. I know it's completely abnormal to wish I could stay after school. Any other day, I'd be beating a path to my locker and rushing outside with Jess and Sara and Amelia, but right now my sneakers are dragging along the speckled linoleum as if they have magnets attached to their soles. Right foot (hot pink shoelace), left foot (pumpkin orange).

Today's my first day at my new sort-of job. I say sort-of because I'm thirteen, which is not legal working age yet for a regular job. But it's fine to "help out" in a family-run business, and Cinderella Cleaners is nothing if not family-run.

First by my grandparents, now by my dad. One of Dad's part-time workers just went off to college, and my step-mother, Fay, convinced him that I should "pitch in."

Not only that, but I have to start work on the very same day that the drama club's holding auditions for the fall play, *Our Town*, by Thornton Wilder. I'm dying to go there with Jess and try out. I know I can't, but some stubborn piece of my brain hasn't given up hope of a last-minute rescue, even though there's no bell to be saved by this time.

Our friend Ethan Horowitz is walking toward our lockers with a new kid named Will Carson, who sits behind me in English class. Will's tall and quiet, but Ethan is loud enough for two. He's got the kind of looks that could go either way — kind of stocky, with sandy brown hair — but he's so sure of himself that everybody just takes it on credit he's cute. "See you guys at auditions," he says with a grin. I've told him three times that I'm not trying out, but apparently it didn't get through the borders of Ethan World.

"You bet," says Jess, and then, so I won't have to tell him *again* — Jess is that kind of friend — she asks Will if he's going to audition.

Will looks a little embarrassed. He shrugs, and his dark hair falls over his forehead. He pushes it back with one hand. "I'm not into acting much. I thought I'd try stage crew."

"Oh, cool!" says Jess. "We can use some new hands on the tech side."

It's hard not to feel left out of that "we." I've been in every fall play since I started middle school. Last year I played Eliza Doolittle in *My Fair Lady*. I spent months watching movies to practice my English accent, and I got to wear this gorgeous ivory ball gown. In sixth grade, we did a musical called *Cafeteria Daze*. I was just in the lunch lady chorus, but even though the show was kind of lame, I was thrilled to be up on the stage with eighth graders. They seemed so grown up.

But this year, I *am* in eighth grade, and I won't even get to try out. Fay's waiting right outside the school in her SUV to make sure I won't "pull any stunts." This is a waste of her time. I've already pulled everything I could pull — I promised my dad I'd work every afternoon *after* the play's done, and weekends, and winter vacation — but Fay thinks I'm old enough to give up things I love.

Well, what can you say to *that*? I can't stand the look on Dad's face when Fay and I get into fights, like his heart's being pulled into pieces, so I just agreed.

Ethan and Will head down the hall, and Jess leans on the lockers, watching me spin the dial on my lock. "It's not *fair*," she says with her lower lip stuck out like a shelf.

"It's okay," I tell her with a sigh. "There'll be other plays."

"If the drama club earns enough money," Jess replies darkly and I nod. Last year's ticket sales didn't cover expenses, so the drama club is in danger of being shut down. I wish I could help out in some way, but I've got to go take care of rich people's clothes.

It isn't as bad as it sounds. When I was little, Cinderella Cleaners was my favorite place in the world. I used to beg my grandpapa to let me stand on the pedal that makes all the clothes circle around the whole shop in their long plastic bags — the Dress Parade, I used to call it. Now I'll be running the Dress Parade. Last winter, Papa and Nonni retired to Miami Beach, and my dad started running the business. I don't think he likes it as much as he liked painting houses, but Dad's never been a complainer.

I open my locker. The inside of the door is plastered with photos of my favorite actors. Johnny Depp, Daniel Radcliffe, Zac Efron, the whole cast of *Twilight*, and my newest celebrity crush, Adam Kessler, whose eyes are as blue as a tropical pool. He just had a small part on *Gossip Girl* and he's playing the lead in a brand-new rock musical that's opening on Broadway next month. It's called *Angel*, and as soon as I saw the commercial for it, I switched the wallpaper on my laptop from Zac to Adam.

Jess looks at his face. "I can't wait to see *Angel*. He is *so* cute." Suddenly she grabs my arm. "Logo alert!"

I look over my shoulder in time to see Kayleigh Carell, wearing the whole Paramus Park Mall. If Kayleigh owns any item of clothing that doesn't say what store it came from, it must be pajamas.

Today she's wearing an Abercrombie cardigan that says ABERCROMBIE, and Hollister sweats that say HOLLISTER. Her cami is subtle: Instead of AMERICAN EAGLE, it just says AE. She's walking with her boyfriend, Zane, and they're holding hands in this annoyingly *look-we're-holding-hands* way. This is what's called "going out" in eighth grade. You don't *go* anywhere. You just walk around holding hands in the hall and tell anybody who'll listen that you're going out. Then you get one of your friends to break up for you during lunch, and go out with somebody else. It's ridiculous.

Kayleigh has already heard I'm not going to try out, so she could afford to be nice to the peasants, but she just pretends to be giggling her head off at something Zane said as they pass by my locker.

"If *she* gets to play Emily," Jess says through clenched teeth, "I will puke."

"Maybe *you'll* get the part," I say, though Emily Webb is the lead role in *Our Town*, and Jess always tries out for comic parts. She was a total tomboy when we were both kids — she beat up all the boys on the playground — and even now she dresses in skateboarder hoodies and skinny jeans, adding a Mad Hatter top hat whenever she can. She'd wear the hat to school if there wasn't a dress code rule about headgear; our principal thinks it encourages gangs. It's hard to imagine a gang sporting Mad Hatter top hats, but if there was, Jessica Munson would rule it.

I have a totally different style. I'm into fashion as much as the next girl, but my thing is vintage. I love prowling through thrift stores and resale boutiques, trying to find buried treasure. I can stop at a yard sale that seems to be nothing but teacups and toddler toys, and sleuth out a pearl-embroidered fifties cardigan that would be *perfect* over a cami, or a hippie-style skirt that's so out, it's back in. If I didn't like acting so much, I'd want to be a fashion designer.

What can I say? I love playing with clothes. In the privacy of my own room, I put together outfits that no one but me could imagine. Only problem is, I'm too self-conscious to wear my best looks to school. Kayleigh and her posse would stare at me like I was wearing a Halloween costume, and even though I know I shouldn't care what they think, it's no fun to have everyone saying you're weird. So I stick to the basic food groups of T-shirts, jeans, and sneakers, and just try to liven things up with accessories. I covered one wall of my bedroom with hooks, and I keep all my earrings and bangles and scarves on display 24/7.

"I've got to roll," I tell Jess. "Break a lemon." I can't remember when we started messing with the old theatre cliché "Break a leg," but now it's tradition. Usually, Jess would respond with a "break a whatever" of her own, but instead she just gives me a sad little smile and a hug.

"I'll tell all tonight," she says. "Text me from the cleaners if you get a chance."

Fay is parked in the Staff Only section, right in front of a sign that says GUIDANCE. Either she didn't bother to read it or she's given herself a new title. She's left her SUV running, of course, with the A/C on. She's madly in love with her new car, and thinks global warming is nonsense.

"I have a client in twenty-five minutes," she tells me instead of hello as I get in the passenger seat. "It's a good thing the twins have an after-school playdate."

I wish I *had an after-school playdate,* I think as Fay backs up too fast, nearly clipping somebody's Toyota. Across the parking lot, flocks of kids are climbing onto their school buses, calling and shrieking like birds. Under the pine trees, some slackers are tossing a Frisbee around. A few girls from the soccer team lope onto the field and do stretches. I turn my head, looking for Sara and Amelia, but they must still be inside the locker room.

I try not to think any more about drama club, but I can't help wondering who's going to try out for the role of Emily Webb, or her boyfriend, George Gibbs. Not that the eighth grade has any great guys, but that's why it's called acting: I can be madly in love with a four-foot-tall nerd if you put us onstage. In *Our Town*, George and Emily fall in love and get married, and years later Emily dies, but she gets to come back for just one precious day. It's all done on a bare stage, with a narrator called the Stage Manager telling the story, and it's the best play ever.

"When I was your age, I worked after school *and* on weekends," says Fay, whose nails are a shade of magenta that doesn't occur in the natural world.

Why don't grown-ups get that if you want a kid's ears to shut down, the best way to start is, "When I was your age . . ."? When Fay was my age, there were ground sloths and mastodons. She's gripping the leather-wrapped steering wheel as she heads down the hill toward the river.

Dad married Fay when I was in fifth grade, six months after my mom died. They met in a cancer bereavement support group. I know he was falling apart without Mom, and that I should be happy he found someone, but why did it have to be *her*?

Mom would have let me try out for *Our Town*. And she would have been thrilled if I got the lead. I think of

11

the scene in Act Three where Emily gets to come back from the dead for a day, just one day, and I suddenly realize that my eyes are moist. What would it feel like to look at the actress who's playing Emily's mother and tell her that life goes too fast and we don't get to *look* at each other? It's true, it's all true.

That's what I love about being in plays. It gives you a place to put all the feelings you have every day and can't show to anyone else or they'll think you're emo.

When I was a little kid, I used to pedal my bike around the neighborhood, interviewing myself, just to get into practice. "Oh, yes," I would croon to invisible talk-show hosts, "I've always admired the theatre. My favorite show? There are so many. Either *Annie* or *Chorus Line*." (I thought it was dashing to leave out the *A*.) Once I was telling Oprah how I got my big break as a replacement orphan when Annie came down with the flu. I didn't realize how loud I had gotten till Mrs. Pomerantz looked over her laundry line and said to her cat, "That Diana girl talks to herself."

Fay's driving us right past the Hoboken docks, where they shot *The Sopranos*. She's chatting away on her cell phone, so I get to stare out the window. The Hudson River is choppy today, like the ocean it's meeting. I admire the shapes of the midtown skyscrapers, all different colors and heights like old books on a shelf. Every one of those windows is someone's apartment or office. If you lived in the city, you'd never run out of people to meet. And right in the middle of all those big buildings, carving a long zigzag where everything else is in squares, is Broadway.

I have a *Playbill* for every show I've seen, on the wall of my bedroom. The wall slants right over my bed, so I lie there at night and look, trying to picture myself in each theatre: maroon velvet seats that smell like old curtains, fancy ceilings with gold chandeliers. I think about all the actors who've been on that stage, how they stood in the wings with their hearts pounding, feeling the audience rustle and hush as the lights dimmed to half.

The last show I saw with my mom was *The Lion King*. We loved it so much that we couldn't bear to get up from our seats. We were the last people out of the theatre, except the guy sweeping the aisles. Every time I play the CD, I can feel Mom's fingers twined in mine; and if I have to cry onstage, that's all I need to remember.

• • •

Fay's stopped at a traffic light right down the road from the cleaners. I can see the top of its neon sign over the roofs of the neighboring stores, and the sight makes my heart race a little. I've never had anything like a real job before, just babysitting and yard work for neighbors. This feels really different, much more adult and important. I'm feeling the same kind of pit-of-the-stomach nervous excitement I get when I stand in the wings right before my first entrance.

Maybe the trick is to see this new job as a play I've been cast in. Not the role I was hoping for, but sometimes you have to make do with the role you've been given. And even if Fay was the one who insisted that I start right now, it was Dad who wanted me to come work for him. That's kind of huge.

The traffic light changes to green and we move forward. *This is it*, I think, taking a long deep breath. *This is where everything changes.*

Chapter Two

Cinderella Cleaners isn't as big as my school, but it's built from the same salmon-colored bricks and cement. Weehawken Middle School does not have a neon-lit crown on its roof, though, or signs that say WE DRY-CLEAN EVERYTHING! and YOU GET IT DIRTY AND WE'LL GET IT CLEAN! And the school isn't right next to an old-fashioned chrome diner. It's all pretty strip-malled around here, but Dad says that Cinderella Cleaners and Sam's Diner look just the same as they did when he was a kid.

Fay pulls into a customer parking slot, still on her phone call. She lays her hand over the mouthpiece and whispers, "Your father will drive you home."

I nod and whisper back, "Thanks," as she says to the

headset, "No, nothing." As soon as my feet hit the pavement, she's backing away.

I stand there and look at my future. The window is plate glass, with a crown stenciled right in the center. Looking through it, I see a customer's back and two people standing behind the customer counter. One is a tall teenage girl with straight blond hair, and the other is a thin, sharp, older woman wearing cat-eye glasses that look like they came from the Drama Club props box. I've met her before — she was here when my grandfather managed the cleaners — but I don't remember her name. They're both wearing smocks, the exact shade of pastel mint green that's used for school menus. I always wonder who picked out the colors for copy paper: salmon pink, dull blue, buff, and the most boring green in the world, the only possible way to make fish sticks and chicken parm even *less* appetizing. Would it be such a problem to xerox on teal or pistachio?

As I stand watching, the blond girl turns away from her customer and steps on a pedal, and there goes the Dress Parade, plastic bags swishing as clothes swoop around the room on a conveyor belt. It still feels like magic.

I exhale and step through the automatic door, ringing a bell. The sounds and smells inside are unmistakable. It's easily ten degrees hotter, and there's a rickety clatter of sewing machines from the tailoring section, off to the left, and the clunk of industrial cleaning machines from the back workroom. The Dress Parade stops, and the blonde hands a plastic-bagged suit to her customer. "Have a nice day," she says, smiling, as he turns toward the door, holding the wire hanger over his shoulder.

There's no one else waiting in line, so I walk right up to the customer counter. The cat-eye woman glares at me.

"Hi, I'm Diana," I tell her, and when she says nothing, "Is my father here?"

Behind the bifocal lenses, I see her eyes narrow, and sense an instant dislike clicking into place. The plastic nameplate under the embroidered gold crown on her smock says JOY. *Joy*, I think. Who are they kidding?

"I'll buzz him," says Joyless. But she doesn't have to. The office door swings open, banging against a bulletin board full of posters for local band concerts and bingo nights. Dad comes out, beaming, and folds me against his big chest in a bear hug. His clothes smell like dry-cleaning fluid. When I was little, I would hold my breath every time Papa came near me in one of his gabardine jackets and vintage ties — "Face it, I'm a dresser," he'd say, and grin — but now that I'm deep in the source of that smell, surrounded by chemical cleanliness, it's almost comforting. It smells like family.

"This is my wonderful daughter, who's going to help out in the afternoons," Dad says, flipping up a hinged section of countertop. He turns me around by the shoulders and steers me through. "Meet Joy and Elise."

Elise dips her head with a shy smile. She wears sparkly earrings and looks about sixteen years old, but she's almost as tall as my dad.

"Miss MacInerny," says Joyless, making it clear her first name is off-limits as she pinches my fingers in hers. "I'm the supervisor."

How did I guess? Maybe because she acts like a cross between the Wicked Witch of the West and a lunch lady?

Dad says, "I've got a client on hold. Can one of you girls show Diana around?" MacInerny's frown deepens at the word *girls*, though if I was her age, I'd be grateful.

"I will," Elise offers, and I want to hug her.

"I'll need someone in customer service," MacInerny says. "Catalina is *late*."

"I'm here, I'm here!" pants a short, dark-haired girl as she bursts through the double doors from the back room, still snapping on her smock. "I had to talk to my chem teacher. Sorry. Where do you need me at, computer or cash register? Hey, are you new?" she says, spotting me next to Elise.

I'm glad to see someone else close to my age; Catalina looks as if she's in high school. "I'm Diana," I tell her.

"Cat," she says, flashing a mischievous grin that means *Catch you later, okay?* In the next instant, she's greeting an old lady who steps up to the counter, clutching her pink pickup slip in one hand. "Hey, Mrs. Litzky, you back for that raincoat already? Nice beads! Are those from your daughter?" The old lady beams as if Cat's her best friend.

Elise looks at me. "Are you going to work at the counter like me and Cat?"

Joyless jumps in. "Not at the cash register. She's too young." She shoots me a look. "You'll be tagging and sorting and bringing clothes back to the workroom. Stains go to Special Care, alterations to Tailoring."

Tailoring! That could be cool. Maybe I'll pick up some fashion design tips.

Elise shows me how garments get logged in on the computer, then tagged with a wire through the label that won't come off in the machines. Everything's numbered, and coded by color. Next she takes me to the tailoring section, to the left of the customer counter. Here, the sewing machines' clatter sounds like typewriters. There are racks of bright-colored thread all down one wall, a few dress-maker's forms, and a small curtained fitting room next to a three-way mirror.

I catch a glimpse of myself, with my graywash jeans, black Converse, and dark purple T-shirt reflected in many directions. I guess I was depressed about missing auditions when I picked out my outfit this morning — I look like a bruise. Even my earrings are boring: plain silver hoops. I remind myself not to ignore the accessory wall in my bedroom. Clothes have to make *some* kind of statement, but today's is, "Don't bother to look at me."

Two tailors, both elderly women, are smiling at me from their sewing machines, where they're hemming identical peach bridesmaids' dresses. "You don't remember us, do you?" says the whiter-haired one, in the kind of New Jersey accent that might cut through glass. "I'm Loretta, that's Sadie. You must be Frank's daughter."

"Of course she's his daughter," rasps Sadie. "I'd know those eyes anywhere."

Loretta sits back, her lap full of peach ruffles. "Your grandfather used to bring you in when you were just a little peanut, and look at you now! You got so *tall*."

I smile self-consciously. Why does every adult on earth have to comment on this? Do they think kids are going to get shorter? It's called growing *up*.

"Where's Nelson?" Elise asks.

Sadie shrugs. "Out buying more lace," says Loretta. "These bridesmaids are gonna look like Little Bo Peep."

Elise touches a ruffle. "Did Nelson design these?"

"Bite your tongue," says someone behind me. "Those weren't designed, they fell off a parade float."

I turn to see a tall guy in a hip-hop fedora and vest, striding in with a large paper bag. This must be the head tailor, Nelson Martinez. I've heard my dad talk about him.

Frowning, Nelson upends the bag onto the cutting table, dumping out several spools of lace trim.

"Client wants lace, we sew lace." Sadie shrugs. "That's why they pay us the big bucks."

Loretta jumps in before Nelson can answer. "This is Diana Donato. Frank's daughter."

Nelson casts an appraising eye over my outfit. I can sense his disdain as he gives a curt nod. I wish I'd worn something with more style. When it becomes clear he's not going to speak, Loretta tilts her head toward the garment rack.

"We got two of these done, if you girls want to tag 'em and bag 'em."

"Great," says Elise. "That'll be our next stop." She picks up a finished peach gown, lifting it high to protect the hem, and I do the same, feeling the weight of the shimmery fabric against my arm. We go back to the customer counter, circling behind Joyless and Cat.

"Is that cart good to go?" Elise asks, and Cat says, "Be my guest." Elise hooks the rolling cart with her free hand and backs through the double doors, smooth as a waitress with arms full of trays. She holds the door open for me with one hip.

The back room is three times the size of the customer area. There are workers bent over steam-pressing machines and carrying armloads of clothes. It looks like a Laundromat on steroids. Big cleaning machines spin and clunk as clothes bagged in plastic swish by overhead. There might be a radio playing, but there's so much machine noise, it's hard to make out. It's all I can do not to cover my ears.

"You get used to it," Elise shouts. We carry the brides-maid gowns to a garment rack next to a bagging machine with a huge roll of plastic above, like a supersize version of the ones in the ShopRite produce aisle. A wiry African-American guy is up on a ladder, replacing the roll.

"Boss's daughter?" He grins. "I heard about you."

Seems like everyone has. I can't help wondering how much Dad's been talking about me, and it makes me feel even more shy. "I'm Diana."

He holds out a high five and tells me his name, but it's lost in a sudden thump of machine noise and he has to repeat it. "Chris. Chris like Chris Rock, but not as rich."

Elise and I laugh and continue the tour. She pushes the cart of dirty clothes to a big sorting table in the center of the room. I'm amazed to see so many garments all mixed

23

up together: fringed suede and designer silk, men's shirts and chenille sweaters. If people had any clue how their fanciest clothes get handled behind the scenes, they'd be shocked. Armani suits and Army surplus, cashmere and chintz: Back here, it's all just a bunch of old laundry.

Elise opens the door of a walk-in vault that is blissfully cool. "This is where we store fur coats," she says, wrinkling her nose with distaste and shutting the door before I get to see what's inside.

The old man at the steam presser, Mr. Chen, barely looks up from the trousers he's pleating as he nods a brisk greeting. A small, sturdy woman named Rose is the stain expert; her Special Care workstation looks like a chemistry lab. I'm starting to wonder how many more names I can hold in my head, when Elise brings me into a pale yellow locker room, where it's a little bit quieter.

"This is where we leave our stuff," she says. "Pick any locker that's empty."

I nod, trying my best not to look overwhelmed. It's a bit like the first day at a new school, except everyone else is much older than me, and they already know the routine.

"You'll get it down fast," Elise reassures me. "Basically, all you'll be doing is carrying clothes from one place to another. It's like cleaning your room about six million times."

Wow, that sounds *great*.

"How long have you worked here?" I ask her.

"Two years, on and off. I don't work much during basketball season."

I'm not very good at sports, but I kind of like basketball when we play it in gym. It's better than flag football, anyway. "Are you on a team?"

"Hoboken High," she says with pride. "I'm on varsity."

"Cool."

"It is. It's way cool." She has a nice smile. That girl Cat looked pretty friendly, too. If I like the people I work with, I might start to feel better about having to clean my room six million times.

Elise leads me past the lockers and bathroom stalls and into the back hallway to show me the employee entrance; the front door is for customers only. There's a big sign hanging over the coffee machine:

HAVE YOU SWIPED TODAY???

"Is there a lot of stealing?" I ask. Elise looks confused, so I point at the sign.

She bursts out laughing and says, "Swipe your *card*."

Now it's my turn to look blank. "Your time card." Elise points at the twin rows of slots by the time clock. "Ask your father if you're supposed to get one. And here's where you pick up your smock." She takes a Women's Medium smock off the rack for me. It looks huge, but she tells me the more air around my body, the cooler I'll be. I put my arms into the pastel green sleeves and suddenly feel as if I'm in the costume shop backstage, getting fitted for dress rehearsal. As soon as you're dressed for the role, you can feel the worst parts of you disappear — the clumsy, shy, never-know-what-to-say-next parts. You become someone else, who knows all the right lines.

"Ready?" Elise asks, and we go back into the workroom.

Cat's taken Elise's place at the front counter, logging in orders, circling stains with a fabric crayon, and stapling tags on each garment. She has a wide smile and a breathless

26

way of talking that makes every customer think she's their best buddy, but the comments she makes from the side of her mouth as she tosses their clothes into my cart are hysterical. "Ooh, spandex, thinks she's a hottie . . . You know, this looks *better* with dried marinara sauce."

On the third or fourth trip, I start commenting back, pointing to a stained blazer. "Prada's showing linen with pesto this year."

Cat grins and imitates *Project Runway*'s Heidi Klum. "At Cinderella Cleaners, you're either *in* or you're *out*." The German accent mixed with her slight Spanish inflection makes this even funnier.

MacInerny notices us laughing and gives me the evil eye, so I hustle the cart through the swinging doors into the back room. I wonder if I'll ever get used to the noise level. Most of the workers wear earplugs, which makes me wonder why there's a radio on. Maybe somebody thinks it smooths over the chaos.

Elise waves at me from the bagging machine. "Hey, can you give me a hand sorting orders?"

"Sure thing," I tell her. It's cool to see what goes with what. Some orders are all the same thing — light blue men's dress shirts or flower-print dresses — and some are so varied it's hard to believe the same person dropped off all these garments. I get mental pictures of every customer. Dress For Success Woman, size 6, with shoulder pads on every pantsuit, has *got* to be blond, button earrings, firm hand-shake. Disco Guy wore that white suit to his cousin's Greek wedding and drank way too much wine.

"Having fun yet?" Elise asks, handing over a new load of freshly bagged clothes. To my surprise, the answer is yes. If you squint your eyes sideways, it's not hard to picture this place as the world's largest costume shop.

By closing time, my arms are aching. I never realized clothes were so *heavy*. Elise says this job is her off-season workout for basketball. She's saving up money to go to a basketball camp this summer. She's a little obsessed, like my soccer team friends, but she's really nice. When MacInerny's not looking, Elise and Chris like to jump-shot trash into a basket across the room. Elise never misses a shot.

The back room is finally quieting down as the cleaning machines are shut off for the night. Loretta and Sadie are telling each other what they're going to heat up for dinner.

Mr. Chen, the thin Asian man who's hunched over the steam press in silence all day, hangs up his last dress shirt and straightens up, stretching his arms overhead. Rose, the stain expert, pads over to him, and though neither one speaks as they head for the locker rooms, it's clear from the way their two bodies lean toward each other that they're husband and wife.

"Closing tiiiime!" Chris pretends to be dribbling a ball past Elise, and she swats at him playfully. "Oh, you're too good for me now? Hanging out with the boss's daughter instead of me." He winks at me as he goes past.

"Are you tired?" Elise asks, and I suddenly feel like I've climbed up a mountain. I can't believe it's only been my first day of work, and I can't wait to get into Dad's car.

Chapter Three

As soon as I get home, I close the door to my room and flop down on my bed, speed-dialing Jess on my cell while my laptop boots up. All our friends Facebook, but Jess and I also have a nightly phone call tradition that goes back to grade school. As soon as she picks up, I ask about *Our Town* auditions. Of course, *she* wants to hear all about my first day on the job.

"You didn't text me," she says, and I realize that I forgot.

"Too busy," I say. "It was okay, but my arms are still sore. I'm going to get buff. So what parts did you read for?"

"I totally stunk," she wails. "On a scale of one to ten, I was negative twelve."

"Oh, come on," I say, staring at the Adam Kessler photo on my laptop. "I'm sure you were great."

"I lost my place *twice*. And then I jumped in with a line that was somebody else's. Ms. Wyant will probably cast me as Second Dead Person. Hey, did you write down the math homework? Sara's not home yet, so I couldn't ask her."

"Graphs fifteen to twenty. Did you read for Emily?"

Jess groans. "Are you kidding? The one consolation is Kayleigh was *awful*."

This makes me happier than I can say. "Define *awful*."

"Ham on rye. She was reading with Ethan, and she kept doing this fake-crying sob thing. I thought she had hiccups."

I laugh so hard I practically get hiccups myself. "I totally love you, Jess!"

The next morning, we're actually early for school. Instead of waiting for Sara and Amelia by the flagpole next to the bus stop, we hurry right in. Jess is muttering that she'll be lucky if she's on the cast list at all.

"Shut up or I'll kick you," I say.

"But I was so — OW!!!" Jess glares at me.

"Told you I'd kick you." She swings a hand up to karate-chop me, but I can see she's just kidding. Anyway, we've arrived outside Ms. Wyant's classroom.

The cast list is up on the door, and there's a cluster of backs leaning anxiously toward it. I hear a few moans and a chirpy "Oh, yay!" from some sixth grader who's thrilled to be Lady in Balcony. I play the height advantage, leaning over a chipmunk-cheeked boy who comes up to my chin. I see Riley Jackson is playing the narrator role called the Stage Manager, and Ethan is playing George Gibbs. And there it is, in hideous black and white:

EMILY WEBB...................................Kayleigh Carell

Talk about having to give up things you love. This is harsh.

"What?" Jess says, craning. And then we both see: Jess has been cast as Emily's mother. "You've got to be kidding."

"It's a good role," I tell her, but I can see from the set of her jaw that she's not having any of it. She stomps down the hall, red hair bouncing. It's all I can do not to shout at her back, "At least you're in the *play!*"

Two days later, Dad comes to pick me up at school because Fay's showing a waterfront condo to one of her clients and they're running late. "You two don't have to pick me up after school every day," I say. "I can ride the bus to the cleaners."

Dad frowns. "I don't like to think of you taking public transit."

"Not *that* bus, the school bus. I can get on a route that goes all the way down to the cleaners. I rode it last year when I did that science fair project with Amelia Williams, remember? I picked up a bus pass for you to sign."

We're at a stoplight, and dad turns to look at me. "When did you get so grown up?" he says, and his eyes look darker and bigger than usual. I have the sudden sensation that he's going to start crying, but thank goodness he doesn't. "I know how much you wanted to be in the play," he says, looking right in my eyes. "I wish — "

"The light's green," I tell him, nodding my head toward the windshield as the car behind us starts honking. He takes his foot off the brake and pulls out into traffic, leaving his sentence unfinished. I wonder what he would have wished, but decide not to ask.

What do *I* wish? That's a question with too many answers.

Fay serves lasagna for dinner. She always tries to make dishes Dad likes, but she should steer clear of Italian food. My nonni was born in Italy, and she taught Mom to make the best red sauce ever, boiling down bushels of farm stand plum tomatoes with basil Mom grew in our yard. Every time I chew on something Fay poured from a jar, I feel sad in the pit of my stomach. But nothing tastes right tonight anyway. My head is so full of dry-cleaning smells that everything seems to be wrapped up in plastic.

The twins are sitting across from me. Ashley is tracing a pattern of leftover sauce on her plate with her fork, and Brynna's scraping the extra cheese from the rim of the casserole and picking it up with her fingers. If I did that, I'd be busted for manners, but Fay doesn't say a word. When I was little, I used to dream about having a sister. Now I have two, and I'm here to tell you, never complain about being an only child.

"Did you get me that DVD?" Ashley asks at the same time that Brynna pipes, "What's for dessert?" They're about to turn nine, and they both have blond hair and blue eyes; their friends call them Hannah Montana. They aren't identical twins, but sometimes the only way you can tell them apart is that Brynna looks friendlier. Ashley, who's ten minutes older and thinks she's the boss, is already sending off popular-girl disdain vibes and she's only in the third grade.

"Homework first," Fay says briskly. "And dishes."

"Dishes" means me, of course. Ashley and Brynna, whose homework might take them all of ten minutes, are too young for chores.

As I pick up the casserole dish and start stacking plates, I wonder how Cat would describe Fay's olive-and-beige patterned blouse if it came in over the counter. I can hear her breathy voice in my ear, whispering, "That blouse was marked down for a *reason*, okay?" and I can't hold back a smile.

• • •

It's Saturday morning already. Somehow my first week of working went by really fast, but it's great to be a free agent again. I ride my bike over to Jess's house, which is only a few blocks away but on much higher ground than ours. Usually when I hit the long hill, I have to get off and push, but I already feel like I'm getting stronger. I shift to the lowest gear and huff away. Sure enough, I make it up to the top. Yes!

I turn to look out at the city. The river is glassy and smooth today, almost as blue as the September sky. There's the usual snarl of cars inching their way toward the Lincoln Tunnel. I bet a lot of the drivers have tickets for Broadway matinees. A helicopter swoops overhead, and I picture a frosted blonde with a microphone giving a traffic report. "Conditions are slow at the tunnel. Expect delays."

The entrance ramp curls around like a snail, with an unlikely softball field perched in the center. Two Little League teams are trading positions and I wonder if Jess's kid brother, Dash, is playing. I squint at the outfield, looking for telltale red hair. Someone taps on my shoulder and I jump a mile.

"Gotcha!" says Jess, laughing under her top hat. "Spaced out much?"

"You stink!" I fake a punch at her arm, but I'm laughing, too. Jess is on foot, so we walk side by side as I push my bike. I notice that she still won't step on the cracks in the sidewalk. Actors are more superstitious than anyone. It's even bad luck to say "Good luck," which is why we say "Break a leg" or our own variations on breaking whatever sounds good. I'm glad to see Jess is wearing the earrings I gave her on her last birthday, little clusters of silver stars.

"You won't believe all the *drama* in drama club," she tells me. "Kayleigh's quote 'boyfriend'?"

"Zane?"

"Zane the Insane. He found out her character gets married to Ethan in the play and he's having a fit. Threatened to break up if she has to kiss the groom."

"Does she?" I hope so. I'd love to see Kayleigh get dumped.

"The wedding scene hasn't been staged yet. Major suspense."

"If you had to kiss one of them —"

"I'd lose my lunch," says Jess. "Ew!"

"If you *had* to. Onstage. Which one?"

Jess ponders a minute, then shrugs. "I guess Ethan. Zane is a jerk. Oh, yeah, and the sophomore playing the milkman? He got suspended for leaving a hot dog in somebody's gym locker. Inside his sneaker."

"That's so gross! And awesome!"

"I know, right? Other than that, things are groovy."

"*Groovy?* You are so retro."

"I try." We're cutting across the parking lot of the grocery store on the corner, and as I push my bike past a truck at the loading dock, a long train of shopping carts nearly plows into it.

"Sorry!" The tall, lanky kid who was pushing the carts bites his lip with embarrassment. It's Will, from my English class.

"Good one!" says Jess.

"Didn't see you," he says, dipping his head. His dark hair falls into his eyes again. Some guys do that *I-don't-care-what-I-look-like,-okay?* thing, but you know they spent just as long messing their hair up and picking the right baggy T-shirt as Kayleigh does matching up labels. But

Will doesn't seem to be copping an attitude, just wearing clothes that he's comfortable in: black jeans, Converse high-tops, and a rust-colored tee with an old Beatles graphic. Ethan told me his family moved here from New Mexico. Talk about culture shock. Pueblos to Pizza Hut.

"So do you work here?" asks Jess, though the answer is obvious.

"Weekends, yeah. I'm trying to buy a new bass."

"Bass guitar?" Jess sounds very impressed.

Will gives a shy shrug, like it's no big deal. He glances at my bright red earrings and vintage scarf, not quite meeting my eye, and says, "Gotta get these inside. See you." He steers the first cart's handle to the right, and the rest curve away like a long metal worm, clanking over the asphalt as he lopes away. I start rolling my bike again.

"Will joined the stage crew," says Jess. "He's going to run sound."

"Sound? That's kind of funny, since he never talks."

Jess nods with a funny half smile. "You didn't notice it, did you? He *likes* you."

"What?" I'm so astounded I stop my bike. "That is ridiculous!"

"It was so obvious."

"How? He said half a sentence. 'Gotta get these inside.'" I drop my voice to a low monotone, making Will sound like a zombie. I can't believe Jessica Munson is saying this. Jess thinks the whole crush and going-out thing is a big waste of time. It's one thing to put photos of the Jonas Brothers on your bedroom wall (Jess) or Adam Kessler inside your locker (me) but crushing on eighth-grade boys, thirteen-year-old humans you've actually *met*, is a whole different thing. The last time I fell for a boy in my class was when Dylan Katz gave me his big sister's ring in first grade and then took it back when she found out he'd stolen it out of her purse. I was heartbroken.

But eighth-grade boys? Not on a bet. This is one of the major things Jess and I have in common. Or had. Maybe the Kayleigh/Zane kissing drama is rubbing off on my best friend, the last girl I know who's not totally boy-crazy.

I like my dramas onstage, thank you very much. Not in the ShopRite parking lot.

Chapter Four

During the next three weeks, I settle into a regular routine, riding the after-school bus to the cleaners. I've found out my job has some perks, including the No Pickup rack at the back of the storage room. When a garment's not claimed within thirty days, it's taken down from the Dress Parade and moved onto the rack. After sixty days, it goes to the Salvation Army. Employees get first dibs, of course, and there's lots of free shopping before things get shipped off. Right now the rack features everything from suit jackets to velvet curtains. For me, it's a treasure trove. I already have my eye on a black satin blouse and two scarves.

I also love working with Cat and Elise. Elise is soft-spoken and endlessly patient, and Cat is a riot. Her mom is from Guatemala, so she speaks both Spanish and English.

41

She makes jokes in both languages, too, since a lot of the workers are Latin American. When I look at her for a translation, she just shrugs and says, "You hadda be there." For the four hundredth time, I wish I was studying Spanish in school, but my mom dreamed of going to Paris and ordering croissants in French, so that's what I took.

Cat's saving up for a car. She's three years older than me and comes up to my shoulder, even wearing the heels she throws into her locker when she gets to work. She calls the hot-pink Crocs she wears at the customer counter "los uglies."

"So why do you wear them?"

"Are you kidding me? They're so comfortable I want to marry them."

"Don't tell your boyfriend." Cat's already shown me his photo on her phone. He's on the wrestling team, a blond with big arms and an *I-think-I'm-hot* smirk.

Cat laughs. "Yeah, Jared? He'd probably be jealous of shoes. Hey, check *this* out." She picks up a powder blue jacket with shiny lapels and points at a chalk-circled stain on the collar. "Guy who dropped this off mentioned the lipstick three times. Bet you it's not his wife's color."

Of course MacInerny is heading our way and hears us both laughing. "This isn't a *club*," she snaps. Behind her, Nelson rolls his eyes at Cat.

Cat and I have created a group of hand signals to give fashion ratings to garments when MacInerny's in earshot. Most are variations on thumbs up, down, or sideways, but we've added a couple of twists. There are many more thumbs down or sideways than up.

At least until the Monday when we get The Dress.

Cat's working alone at the customer counter when somebody drops it off, and when I bring my cart to the front for a load, her eyes are wide.

"We just got a total thumbs-over-the-top. Check it out." I follow her eyeline and gasp. There's a mound of what has to be silk charmeuse on the counter, the most gorgeous chocolate color with bronze overtones. The bodice is gathered into a front-halter neckline with darker lace trim. I've never seen anything so elegant in my life. It looks like a costume from some thirties movie.

"Who dropped it off?" I gasp.

"Very thin woman with sunglasses. What do you bet she's a model?"

I pick up the dress. The fabric feels cool to the touch, like running water.

"It's going to Tailoring," Cat says. "It's got a big split at the waistband and needs a new zipper. Nelson'll love it."

Nelson Martinez can sew, fix, or redesign anything, and does so with life-and-death intensity. He runs the tailoring shop like a chef in a four-star restaurant, going into fits of temper when anyone fails to live up to his standards. Loretta and Sadie just ignore his explosions. "Calm down, you'll live longer," Sadie says.

Nelson and Cat adore each other, maybe because they both grew up speaking Spanish at home — Nelson's family is Cuban — or because they're both addicted to *Project Runway*. Nelson's gone to the open casting calls twice, and he swears he won't stop until he's a contestant. "And if you think I'll stop then, you're crazy," he says. "I'm going to show my collection at Fashion Week, and I'm going to *win*."

Ever since that first time we met, I've gotten the sense Nelson doesn't like me. Maybe it's because Cat and I are so tight, or maybe it's the same "boss's daughter" reaction I've gotten from some of the other workers. What do they think, I'm a management spy? I'm thirteen, hello. Anyway my dad is the best boss anybody could have. I'm starting to think the main reason he needs me to help out is that he gives people so many days off for family time that we're always short-staffed.

Whatever the reason, Nelson always looks like he wishes I wasn't around. But I'm convinced anyone with his fashion sense is going to flip out when he sees The Dress, so I tell Cat I'll bring it to Tailoring.

Nelson's bent over the cutting table, working his pinking shears around a tight corner. He straightens when he sees me come in with The Dress.

"Oh my god, it looks like Halle Berry's Oscar gown. Where did *that* come from?"

"The customer counter," I say like a moron as he pulls it out of my arms.

"No one in Weehawken sold her this dress," Nelson says with authority. "This is couture." He turns it over, running his hand down the rift in the slinky brown fabric. "Split zipper *and* waistband. Looks like somebody overdid the crème brûlée."

"Not a maternity dress," I suggest, getting into the spirit.

Not only does Nelson not laugh at my joke, he fixes me with that same *who-asked-you?* glare he gives me whenever I try to join conversations between him and Cat. Maybe it *is* because my dad's the boss. Anyway it makes me mad. What did I ever do to him except try to be friendly?

"You're welcome," I say, stomping back to the counter. I grab my cart and push it back into the workroom, where no one will ask any questions and I know Elise will be nice to me.

The next day, Dad has an after-work errand in Jersey City. I'm supposed to go with him, but Cat says she'll give me a ride home instead. Her boyfriend, Jared, has lent her his van. The words *boyfriend* and *van* do not mix well with Dad. He leans back in his desk chair and gives us the eye.

"I'm a really safe driver," Cat insists. "I got an A-plus in driver ed."

"Please?" I beg. Dad looks about to say no, so I press the one button that always makes parents obey. "I need extra time for my homework."

"I guess it's all right," Dad says gruffly. "But fasten your seat belt."

"Of course." I kiss his cheek, which feels like sandpaper.

Cat and I get changed in the locker room with Elise and walk out the back door. Elise wears a pink sweat suit and Pumas. She runs three miles home every day after work. As soon as our feet hit the pavement, she takes off, her ponytail bouncing as she waves good-bye. Cat's wearing heels and a cropped denim jacket. She offers me peppermint gum and I shake my head.

"Thanks anyway."

"Gotta freshen my breath," she says, folding a strip of Dentyne between her glossed lips and chomping down. "I'm picking up Jared from wrestling practice." A beaten-up hunter green van sits at the far end of the parking lot. I notice the way Cat moves in high heels as she walks to the side of the van. It's a runway sashay on a five-foot-tall girl with extremely short legs, but she makes it work. It's weird to be hanging around with someone old enough to have a real boyfriend, one who owns his own van.

Cat opens the driver's-side door and gets in. I open the passenger door, feeling very grown up.

"Seat belt," says Cat, pulling on her own. I buckle up and she starts the van, checking both mirrors and backing up carefully. While we wait for a break in traffic so she can pull out of the parking lot, she clicks on the radio. An old song by Rihanna comes through the speakers.

Cat whoops and cranks up the volume. "I *love* this song! This is the *best* song to dance to!" She starts singing along, and I join her. We head down the road in a glorious sunset. The sky is deep orange with lavender streaks. If you saw colors like this in a picture, you'd think it was fake.

When my father was still painting houses, he used to let me ride around in his step van on weekends, but this has much comfier seats. They're like armchairs.

"Um-brella," sings Cat, and I echo, "Ella ella." With the sky turning colors above us and all the headlights strobing past, I feel like I'm in a YouTube video. This is a whole lot more fun than waiting for Dad to get done in his office.

Dad, I think. *Homework*. And quick as a flash, I realize I've left my backpack under the customer counter.

"OMG. Stop the car."

Cat's head swivels toward me. "What?"

"Can you please pull over? Please?"

"What's the matter?" says Cat, pulling into a Taco Bell parking lot.

"My backpack. It's got all my homework."

Cat bursts out laughing. "Way to panic, Diana. I thought you were having a heart attack."

I feel really stupid. "It's just, like, I promised my father," I stammer.

"No problem," says Cat. "We'll go back."

She circles around to the exit and puts on her left turn signal. The traffic flows past in a steady stream. We both crane our necks left and right, but there isn't a break. I tell Cat I'm sorry to slow her down like this.

"Relax," she says. "Nothing's on fire."

"Don't you have to get Jared?"

She shrugs. "If I'm late, he'll wait. I'm not gonna make the turn till it's safe."

The song changes. So does the traffic light down the road, but so many cars make the right turn on red that there's still not an opening. The light turns back to green, and Cat purses her lips. "I better go up to the next traffic light." She switches her signal to make a right turn instead. I have an idea.

"You know what, I'll walk back. We've only gone five or six blocks."

"Don't be stupid," says Cat. "How are you gonna get home?"

"I'll catch a ride to the bank with my dad." I unbuckle my seat belt and swing the door open. "We'll do this another day. Thanks!"

I jump down before Cat can protest, and set off down the sidewalk, passing a long strip of fast food, gas stations, and mini-malls. Whoever nicknamed New Jersey the Garden State hasn't done time on *this* road. The Donut State is more like it.

There's a bit of fall nip in the air, and I pick up my pace as I head past the comforting chrome of Sam's Diner and toward Cinderella Cleaners. I notice the neon-lit crown on the roof is switched off, and I suddenly wonder if Dad took off right after we did. There's only one car in the parking lot, and it's not his Honda. Might be overflow from the diner, or someone might still be at work. *Not MacInerny,*

I pray, my heart starting to pound. I run to the front door. It's locked, and the lights are all off. I bang on it anyway, but there's no answer.

I take a step backward. What should I do? If I can just get to my backpack, I'll have bus money, or my cell to call Jess's mom for a ride, but my pockets are empty. I circle around to the employee entrance, whispering, "*Please please please.*"

Yes! It's unlocked. It's a miracle!

Only thing is, I can't find the light in the hallway. As soon as the door swings shut, I realize that it's really dark back here. Quiet and dark.

"Hello?" I call out. "Anyone here?"

No one answers. There's a slight glow from the Pepsi machine in the hall, and an emergency exit light over the locker room door. I feel my way down to the door, and am happy to find a switch next to it. Now there's some light in the hallway at least, and I can see into the locker room, where there's another switch. The overhead fluorescents flicker and hum before coming up full, making the pastel walls glow. The familiar space calms me. I walk past the center bench, passing Cat's locker, Elise's, and mine. At the end of the room, I pause. *Where* are the lights to the workroom?

I push the locker room door open, letting a slant of light into the windowless workroom. It's cavernous, eerily silent, with big machines hulking in every direction. The clothes in their plastic bags overhead rustle like cellophane ghosts. I swallow hard as I stand there and make my eyes trace the shadowy path I walk twenty times every day. Sure, the room will be dark when this door's closed, but there are emergency lights above the fire exit and the swinging doors that lead out to the front. If I can just make it through those to the customer counter, I'll be home free.

I take a deep breath and step out as far as I can before letting go of the door.

When the door swings shut, it's even worse than I thought: The emergency lights throw a faint red glow over the shadows, making everything spooky.

I concentrate hard on making my way toward the emergency light over the doors, taking slow careful steps so I won't bang into anything in the dark. It seems to take me a year, shuffling along with my arms out in front like a sleepwalker. At one point my knee hits something that rolls. I stifle a gasp, realizing it's only a laundry cart. Finally I reach the double doors and push through to the customer counter. After the dark of the workroom, the twilight glow though the front windows seems bright as noon. It's no problem at all to see under the counter and scoop up my backpack.

Breathing a sigh of relief, I slip it onto my shoulder and head for the front door, but stop before pushing it open. What if I set off the burglar alarm? I better go back through the workroom.

This gives me a shudder. I don't want to cross that room in the dark again. I've got my cell phone in my pack, and the display glows a little, but it's not exactly a flashlight beam. There must be a light panel somewhere in here. Maybe it's next to Dad's office, or down by Tailoring.

Tailoring. As soon as I glance that way, something catches my eye. Nelson has finished repairing The Dress, and it's hanging right on the fitting room door, next to the three-way mirror. I can't resist going to see it.

And touch it. That fabric is magical, so smooth and silky. I pick up the hanger and hold it in front of me, checking myself in the three-way. *Come on*, my heart urges me.

You just crossed a workroom alone in the dark, you deserve a reward. Besides, who's going to know?

This is evil, I think as I put down my backpack and take The Dress into the small fitting room. *You're doing an evil thing.* I step out of my jeans and peel off my cardigan and T-shirt, looking up at the plastic-wrapped garments high over my head on the silent conveyor belt. Then I slide the dress over my head and pull up the new zipper that Nelson has sewn in invisibly, perfectly hidden behind the seam. He's really an artist. I kick off my sneakers and step out to take a look.

There I am. Three of me, angled in mirrors. I've never felt so elegant in my life, not even wearing that ivory ball gown in *My Fair Lady*. It's almost like seeing what I might look like if I was a grown-up. A really rich grown-up, with great taste in clothes. Even my face looks more glamorous somehow. I take a deep breath, testing the words "May I have the envelope, please?" when the dresses above my head suddenly swing into motion.

I scream.

From the back room, someone else screams — - definitely too loud for a ghost. "Who's there?" I call out, but the moving conveyor belt drowns out my voice. The dresses swish past overhead as I race out of the dressing room and toward the double doors, my heart pounding. I angle one door open, and there in the fully lit workroom stands Nelson Martinez, one foot on the pedal that runs the conveyor belt. He's clutching his heart.

"You scared me to death," he snaps.

"Me, too." I'm staring at him. Something's different. Instead of the distressed denim vest and black T-shirt he had on all day, he's wearing a burnt orange silk shirt, and I suddenly realize it's the one Cat took in yesterday, from a college professor who told her that he had it handmade in Thailand. The same shirt I handed Elise a few hours ago, when it came out of the cleaning machine with its curry stains gone.

"That shirt," I stammer. "I think it belongs to a customer."

"Yes?" Nelson raises his eyebrows. "And what are *you* wearing?"

I look down at the chocolate gown, blushing. "Next time, lose the sweat socks," says Nelson. "And hang it back up when you're done. The silk wrinkles like crazy."

"I can't believe how well you repaired it," I tell him. "It's *perfect*."

Nelson gives an impatient wave. "Nothing is perfect, Diana. But sometimes things come out just right." He sounds somehow wise, and I smile at him hesitantly. But he's looking up, watching the numbered tags on the dress parade. Suddenly he takes his foot off the pedal, and the conveyor belt grinds to a halt. He reaches up for a tagged bag and slips out a Versace jacket. I remember it well. Cat and I gave it two thumbs way up.

"Our little secret," says Nelson, pulling the jacket on over the silk shirt. It fits him as if it was tailor-made. He pulls down his cuffs, spreads his collar, and flashes me a wicked grin. "I'm going out on the town."

Chapter Five

I spend the whole bus ride home figuring out what to say about being so late. I try texting Jess, but she doesn't answer. In spite of Dad's worries, the public transit bus is clean and uncrowded, and riding it down a road I've known all my life seems like a very minor adventure, especially compared to the one I just had.

I don't like to tell lies, but the truth poses serious problems. If I tell Dad I got out of the van and walked back to the cleaners alone, he'll never let me ride home with Cat again. And how could I tell him the back door was unlocked after hours without getting Nelson in trouble? If I tell the truth, I'll be punished, and Nelson might lose his job. Cat once told me he's saving tuition for grad school, to get his degree in design. I can't take that risk.

Fay, Dad, and the twins are already having dinner when I come in through the back door. "Thank goodness," says Dad, jumping right up to embrace me. He hasn't eaten one bite of his food.

"Where have you been?" Fay demands. "Your father's been worried sick."

"Sorry it took us so long," I say. "It's completely my fault. I forgot my backpack after school and we had to go get it. It's got all my homework inside." I hold my bag up, showing the evidence.

"Cat drove you all the way back to school in that van?" Dad asks, just as I hoped he would.

I hang my head, mumbling, "Sorry." That doesn't actually answer his question, so technically, I'm not lying.

Fay eyes me suspiciously, certain I'm trying to hide something. She doesn't miss a trick. "Why would the school doors be open this late?"

I'm ready for this one, though. "The custodians always work late. So I figured we'd stand there and pound on the windows till somebody heard us. The front door was locked." Well, it *was*. Just not the front door of my school.

"Sit down, eat your pork chops," Dad says. "They're already half cold."

I set down my backpack and take my seat. Ashley wrinkles her nose. "Your clothes smell all stinky."

"It's dry-cleaning fluid. You smell the same thing every night."

"Well, it's gross." Ashley tosses her head, and Brynna lets out a loud giggle that turns to a snort. Welcome home.

After dinner, I want to tell Jess everything, but I don't dare risk being overheard on the phone. Even my laptop's not safe: I wouldn't put it past Fay to try and hack into my Gmail and Facebook accounts. So when Jess calls me up for our usual before-bed conversation, yammering on about who knows their lines and who doesn't and how things are going backstage in this final tech week, all I can say is, "Have I got a story for you!"

"What?" she demands the next morning. She's striding down the big hill to meet me, even though school's in the other direction. Usually when I reach this corner, she's nowhere in sight, and I have to go knock on the door to her kitchen, where Mrs. Munson is frantically packing lunches for Jess and Dash while they slurp their cereal, and Jess is yanking a brush through her tangles, sometimes between bites. "It is totally uncool to leave a friend hanging all night."

"You know Fay," I say. "Walls have ears." Then I tell Jess the whole story, making my cross through the darkened workroom as dramatic as possible. When I get to the part about Nelson, her jaw drops.

"So he's borrowing clothes overnight?"

"You got it."

"And then brings them back the next morning and gets them recleaned. That's hysterical. You ought to try that for Halloween."

"Are you crazy? I love our zombie gym teachers! Anyway, Dad would go postal."

Jess stops walking. "So *that's* why."

"Why what?"

"You said Nelson's always been weird to you, right? I bet he thought you'd tell your father on him."

This makes perfect sense. And now that he knows I won't? Time will tell.

There's a new spring in my step as we walk the rest of the way to school, talking about homework and Mr. Perotta's bad hair day and Kayleigh Carell's wardrobe, just like old times. I feel like I've got two lives now, at the cleaners and at school, and the only place they overlap is . . . well, *me*. Jess has rehearsals every day, so she hasn't been able to visit me at Cinderella Cleaners, and I work after school every day, so I'm missing out on our friends and *Our Town*.

When Ethan and Will catch up with us next to the flagpole, trading rehearsal gossip and cracking up, I feel like I'm hearing dispatches from some other planet.

"Hey — how does Kayleigh high-five?" Ethan holds a hand out to Will, but they both turn their hands without touching, looking off to one side with an "Ick!"

"You *guys*!" Jess nearly falls over with laughter.

"*You* would've kissed me, right, Diana?" says Ethan.

"Onstage and in character, *maybe*."

"You would." Ethan's always been sure of himself. He's a bit of a jerk that way. He and Jess start discussing a scene they're both in, speeding up as they get more excited, and Will lags behind to walk next to me.

"It's too bad you couldn't try out," he says, which might be the longest sentence I've ever heard from him. Even in English class, he's pretty quiet.

"No biggie," I say. "Just a job. You know how it is."

Will nods and falls silent.

"How's the bass fund?" I ask as we head up the stairs.

"Fine," he says. "Good." There's another long pause as we walk toward our lockers. His T-shirt today says Red Hot Chili Peppers, and I notice he's doodled band logos all over his notebook. He must really like music. Maybe it gives him a way not to feel quite so shy, like me when I'm acting.

We get all the way to my locker without one more word. I reach for my lock, and Will flashes a smile. "Nice talking with you," he says.

Right. If you call that talking.

That afternoon, MacInerny puts Cat on the bagging machine and Elise at the customer counter. I'm coming up front for a fresh load of clothes when I notice a man with a salt-and-pepper beard and funky glasses at the customer counter. He's raising his voice.

"She assured me I'd have it *today*."

"I'm sorry, sir. The curry stains must have needed some extra attention." My heart sinks. I can guess who this is, and I just saw his silk shirt on the sorting table, ready to go in for its second cleaning. "It'll be ready for pickup tomorrow."

"Oh, no. No, no, no. I'm flying to San Diego *tonight*, and that shirt is going to be on my body. Is there somebody here who can —"

MacInerny is swooping this way like a crow, but before she can speak, I break in. "Is the shirt that you're looking for orange Thai silk?" I ask, raising my chin.

"Yes," the man says. I see Nelson's neck stiffening over his sewing machine.

"My fault. I got a couple of tags mixed up in the back, but they're cleaning it now. Would you like me to put it on one-hour rush?"

"Thank you," the customer says. "On *your* dime."

"Of course," I say, wondering how much a rush on a silk shirt will cost me.

MacInerny's eyes narrow into an *I'll-get-you-later* squint. Elise just stands gaping at me, like she can't figure out what

I'm doing. Behind their two heads, I see Nelson look over his shoulder and blow me a kiss.

Elise, Cat, and I get a ten-minute break every afternoon, and though we're not all supposed to take it at the same time, we manage to overlap. Sometimes we go to Sam's Diner next door, but our favorite spot is on the roof, under the neon crown. Elise spotted the rung ladder behind the Dumpster when she was out back doing stretches. It must have been put there so people could climb up to service the big ventilators and fix neon tubes in the crown. The roof is flat and the size of a basketball court, with a pebbly texture. The view is sensational.

It's raining today, though, so Elise and I head for my second favorite place: the fur storage vault. No matter how hot the workroom might get, it's always cool back there. Even better, it's totally private. One time we ran into Chris, flirting by cell with his girlfriend, who works at the airport, but other than that, no one ever sets foot in this room. You just have to sneak in when nobody's watching the door.

"Why did you offer to pay for that rude guy's silk shirt?" Elise asks. "Were you covering for Cat?"

Close enough, I think as I search through the racks. "Kind of. Hey, look at this jacket. Blond mink."

"I hate fur," says Elise.

"I hate the *idea* of fur. But it's so glamorous. Who do you think this belongs to?"

Elise shrugs, uninterested. "Someone who doesn't mind minks getting killed."

Cat is a whole lot more fun at this game. When we came here last week, she picked out a fur-collared black velvet cape and pretended she was a vampire. I put on a dyed-rabbit jacket and did my best Jersey accent ("Yo! Lookit my fuh!"). Maybe there's something new on the rack. I spot a few coats tagged with pink slips, which means they came in for a cleaning, not off-season storage. Nothing weird, like the coat with the bright blue fox collar that's been here for weeks, but there is a breathtaking dark-colored coat I don't recognize.

"Ooh, look at *this*. Is it sable?"

"Who knows," sniffs Elise.

I run my hand over the coat. The pelts are sewn and pieced on a diagonal, very couture, and the shiny dark fur is incredibly soft. Someone with serious money wears this to the opera, or to fashion shows in Paris. She probably lives in the penthouse of one of those river-view condos, with the Chrysler Building as her night-light. I'm picturing upswept dark hair and a very long neck. I slide my arm into one sleeve, trying to get into character. As I wrap myself in the sable coat's generous drape, I can feel my posture elongating, my feet turning out like an aging ballet dancer. Russian.

"You must make the pliés from the top of your head, like a string pulling upvard. It is more zan ze knees vich create the plié."

The door bangs open, and I whip around so fast that I almost knock over Cat, who's coming in. "Hey, minks, you came in here to chill?" she asks, laughing.

I let out a huge sigh of relief, and Elise says, "You almost gave our prima donna a heart attack."

"Prima *ballerina*, dollink." I sweep grandly back into character, striking a pose.

"MacWitch wants you back on the customer counter," Cat tells Elise. "Whoa, that is some coat."

"Vas a gift from a prince," I say, sliding my hands into the pockets. My right hand touches paper. There's something tucked under the lush satin lining, a hidden pocket. "Hey, look at this." My voice is my own. Elise turns at the door as I pull out a cream-colored envelope with the name MARION lettered in red.

"What is it?" breathes Cat.

"I don't know. Should I open it up?"

"We're supposed to turn everything in," says Elise. "Whoever did intake on this wasn't doing their job."

"Wasn't me," says Cat. "I'd remember that coat. See what's in it."

"We're supposed to —"

Cat cuts Elise off with an impatient wave. "Come on, who's gonna know? Is the envelope sealed?"

I check. The flap's unattached; someone's already opened it.

"Cool!" says Cat. "Gimme."

I reach inside and feel . . . tickets. A shape I'd know anywhere. Two theatre tickets and some kind of card. I pull them all out and gasp.

"OMG!"

"What?" says Cat, big-eyed.

"I'm going back out," Elise says, without touching the door.

"It's two tickets for *Angel*! For opening night!" Cat and Elise both look blank, and it's all I can do not to yell at them. How can they not have heard of *Angel*, the hottest musical opening on Broadway? The tickets have been sold out for months. And it stars *Adam Kessler*!

"What's the card say?" asks Cat, and I turn it over.

> *You are cordially invited*
> *to celebrate the opening of*
> ***Angel***
> *VIP Gala at Tavern On The Green*
> *New York, NY*

I can't read any more. My eyes have gone blank in my head.

Oh. My. God. Ohmygod ohmygod. It's an invitation to the opening-night party after the show! My heart starts to race as Cat grabs the card.

"VIP gala — whoa! This is on *Friday*!" We look at each other.

"You have to turn that in," says Elise firmly. "Give it to me."

"Let me call the customer. Please?" I just want to talk to somebody who's going to be there. I've been reading about this show online for months. It's a Wild West story line with a rock sound track, like *Rent*.

And the star's photo is inside my locker!

I hang up the sable and leave with Elise. Cat yells plaintively after us, "What about *my* break?" but I want to talk to this Marion person ASAP.

"Look her up on the customer database and slip me the number," I beg Elise. "I'll get MacInerny into my dad's office."

"How?"

"I'll think of something."

Elise looks at me skeptically. "You're already treading thin ice with that one-hour cleaning job."

Score! "*Thank* you," I say. I'll tell dad that I offered to pay for the orange silk shirt, and Miss MacInerny's upset that I overstepped my bounds. Then he can talk to her while I overstep them again.

MacInerny is not pleased to see us together. "You're late," she snarks at Elise. There are four customers standing in line, and Elise jumps right in at the computer. A few minutes later, when I bring my empty cart back for a refill, she slips me a Post-it note with Marion Lavin's home and cell numbers.

The timing is perfect. Cat just finished bagging the recleaned orange shirt, so I bring it into Dad's office and tell him what happened, making sure to add a tremulous quake to my voice so he thinks I'm afraid MacInerny is mad at me. He calls her inside to discuss it in private.

I leap into action, whipping out my cell and dialing the home phone.

"Lavin residence," answers a dignified voice. I've seen enough movies to know it's the housekeeper.

I lower my own voice to sound older. "May I speak to Marion, please?"

"I'm sorry, she's out of town."

"Should I try her cell?"

There's a slight hesitation. "They're on a plane to Dubai, but I'm sure she'll check messages once she's in flight."

In-flight phones! How jet-set! "Could you please tell her . . ." Impulsively, I change my mind. "How long will she be out of town?"

"Ten days."

I look at the tickets clutched in my hand, and the date seems to vibrate in front of my eyes. Friday is three days away. And the owner will be in Dubai.

A dream's taking root in my brain. Do I dare?

Somehow I keep my voice calm and adult, telling the housekeeper I'll leave a message on Marion Lavin's cell. Not a moment too soon, either — MacInerny is coming out of Dad's office. I hang up quickly, shoving the tickets back into my pocket as I push my cart back to the workroom.

I can't believe that I'm holding two tickets to *Angel* — not only the show, but the opening-night party!

I know it's insane, wrong, and everything else, but all I can think of is:

How can I get there?

This is so bad. I've bent a few rules, told a few not-quite-truths to Dad and a few more to Fay. But I've never done anything like this before. New York City, at night?

But it's *Angel*! It's Adam! Life just doesn't happen like this. This is beyond-wildest-dreams time.

I have to at least try to get there. But who would I take?

Jess is the obvious choice. She would kill to see *Angel* . . . but Friday is opening night of *Our Town*. They're in tech rehearsals right now, probably running the wedding (with a kiss on the cheek at the altar; Kayleigh's still refusing to kiss Ethan, though rumors are flying that she's going to do it on opening night). Anyway, how on earth would we get to New York by ourselves?

Sometimes it really stinks being thirteen years old. But maybe if Cat or Elise could go? They're both over sixteen. They've got driver's licenses.

I think about this for a minute. I absolutely can't see Elise going through with it. Except for sneaking up onto the roof, she's a total good girl. She does all her homework, she gets good grades, she's never late for work. If she wasn't so nice, it would be irritating.

Cat, on the other hand . . . Cat loves a party. She's not into theatre like I am, but she loves music and dancing, and any excuse to dress up. It's worth asking.

She's running clean clothes through the bagging machine, and I join her to bunch and hang up the orders.

"So?" She grins. "Did Marion Sable Coat give you a tip for returning her tickets?"

"She's in Dubai till next week." I give her a meaningful look on *next week*.

"Holy cow! Isn't Dubai, like, in Asia?"

"It's far. Middle East."

"You thinking what I'm thinking?"

"I think I might be." We look at each other.

"A Broadway opening!" Cat exclaims. "You might get to walk the red carpet."

"What red carpet?" a voice says behind us. I turn, and there's Nelson in one of his hipster outfits, crushed hat and suspenders, on his way back from the men's room. Cat launches into a torrent of Spanish. The only words I catch are *Angel*, with an *h* sound (*an-hel*), and *boletas*, which sounds like the French word for tickets, *billets*.

Nelson turns to me. "Go for it. Fell in your lap, meant to be."

"Yeah, but how would I get to New York?"

Nelson waves one hand dismissively. "Listen, you know how to think on your feet. You aced that Thai shirt problem. You'll make it work."

"You can't let those tickets just go to waste," Cat says. I can feel my heart starting to pound, but I make one last effort to do the right thing.

"Why don't you go with Jared?" I ask Cat. "He's got a van."

Cat bursts out laughing. "You don't know Jared. The day he sits still for some musical, pigs will grow wings. Maybe if you found some Knicks tickets."

"So go with Diana," says Nelson, impatient. "It's obvious. Duh! And I can't *wait* to dress you both."

Chapter Six

I know Jess will kill me if I pull "have I got a story" again, so even though I'm dying to tell her about *Angel*, I keep my mouth shut during our nightly phone call. This is not hard, since the *Our Town* opening is three nights away, and true to form, everything's going wrong. Ethan keeps trying to kiss Kayleigh, so at last night's run-through, the wedding scene ended with the bride turning away from the groom, one hand over her mouth. And poor Will played a sound cue of a rooster instead of the funeral bells, which cracked up the whole cast.

"And," says Jess, pausing dramatically, "we've hardly sold any tickets."

I know what this means, and my heart sinks. "So there might not be a spring show?"

"You got it. Unless we get can get some more people to come to this turkey."

"Is *anything* good?"

Jess pauses. "Riley. I was listening to his opening monologue for the third act last night, and I got tears in my eyes. Is that stupid or what?"

"You're supposed to get tears in your eyes. It's a *funeral*."

"The way it looks now," Jess says darkly, "the whole play's a funeral. You *can't* come on opening night. Promise you'll wait till the second weekend?"

How convenient is *that*? I look at the photo of Adam and thank my stars.

The next morning, Jess is late to meet me at our corner, so I have to go to her house. Mrs. Munson, dressed in her nurse's uniform, is hastily making two PB&Js. Jess can't find her Spanish homework, and Dash is still in his pajamas.

Her mom ends up driving us, and we tear into school as the bell rings, so I don't get to tell her about *Angel* till we meet in the hall after homeroom.

Jess's eyes are huge. "I can't *believe* this! Why didn't you tell me last night?"

"Are you kidding? If Fay overheard a word of this, I would be grounded so fast you'd get dizzy. And I'm sure she spies on my laptop."

"You *have* to go. Have to."

"But how?"

"Give me till lunch," Jess says. "I'll think of something." She goes into first-period science and I head for gym, which is not my idea of how any day should begin. Especially when my gym locker's right next to Kayleigh's and her friend Savannah's, and the popular girls stare at my mix-and-match socks like I came from the moon. At least Amelia is in my class, too, though she actually *likes* calisthenics, which I think is weird.

Later, Jess and I meet in the cafeteria line but don't breathe a word till we get past the lunch ladies. We usually sit with Amelia and Sara and some of the drama club kids, but not today. This is completely top secret. It's breezy outside, but we carry our trays to a bench at the edge of the yard.

"Simple," says Jess when we finally sit down. "Tell your dad that you're coming to opening night of *Our Town*. There's a cast party after, and you're sleeping over at my house."

That's pretty brilliant. It's almost not even a lie, except for the name of the play I'll be at. And the opening night party being a VIP gala in New York City instead of a pot-luck at school. But the sleepover part, that should work like a charm. I can sneak into Jess's house late, when Cat and I come back from the city. My heartbeat speeds up. This might actually *work*.

Our next class is computer lab, where we're working in teams. When Mrs. Quinn sits down to show some-thing to Ethan and his partner in the far corner, Jess logs us onto the Web site for *Angel*. We both know the URL by heart.

The new promo's amazing, even more than the first one I've already memorized. The dancing and costumes are stunning, and when the camera swoops in for a close-up of Adam, I feel something flutter deep inside my chest, and forget to breathe.

"Are you okay?" Jess asks, "Your ears are bright red."

"I'm *fine*," I say, getting my breath back in order.

Jess stares at the screen, looking wistful. "I can't believe you get to see this in real life," she says.

That makes two of us.

Cat's as excited as I am. She's already asked Jared if he'll drive us into the city and back. "He can go to a movie or hang at the Hard Rock Cafe. He'll be fine." We agree not to say a word about it to anyone except Nelson, who's doing our outfits.

"How about Elise?"

Cat considers. "Elise wouldn't bust us. She'll tell us we're out of our minds, but she's not gonna bust us."

"We are totally out of our minds," I say.

Cat grins. "Isn't it great?"

MacInerny is on me today like a hawk on a sparrow. She's not at all pleased that my dad had that talk with her, so I'm on best behavior. Even when someone drops off an aqua-and-gold vinyl jacket that needs a new lining, Cat and I don't say a word.

Nelson is not so discreet. When I bring it to Tailoring, he holds it away at arm's length. "Ugh. Someone's missing their swimming pool cover."

"*Don't*," I hiss, swallowing laughter. "I'm being so good today."

He pushes me forward, into earshot of Miss MacInerny, and looks me up and down. "How tall are you, five feet six?"

"Almost," I say. "More like five feet five and a half."

"Perfect," he says, and to Miss MacInerny, "I'm going to borrow Diana. That wedding dress I'm altering, pre-owned, with the extra-long train the bride wants removed? I need a live model to get the drape right."

MacInerny purses her lips. "Can't you use somebody else?"

"Elise's got six feet of shoulders and Cat is pocket-size. Unless *you'd* like to model?"

MacInerny looks as if she'd like to skewer him. Nelson smiles at her sweetly and takes me back into the Tailoring section, where he hands me what looks like twelve yards of white satin. "Sort out this monster and put it on," he says, steering me into the fitting room.

"I need your measurements for the Opening Night Challenge."

It's a chore to sort out all the layers of petticoat, lace, and train and get into the dress in the cramped fitting room. The oversize bodice is studded with seed pearls and sequins, so it seems to weigh about fifty pounds. I have new respect for brides. By the time I step into the Tailoring shop, I'm exhausted.

Loretta and Sadie stop working, holding hands over their hearts as if I'm a real bride. "Oh, she looks beautiful. Doesn't she?"

"You're a vision," says Sadie, her New Jersey accent so thick you could slice it like brisket. "Ya gonna break hearts, mark my woids."

Behind MacInerny's back, Cat flashes two thumbs way up over her head, like an Olympic judge.

I look at myself in the three-way mirror. The bodice is swimming on me, but the swirling pieced skirt and long satin train are right out of a fairy tale. I can see why this woman decided to have it remade. Nelson is looking at me the way a sculptor might look at a fresh block of marble. He circles me, muttering, touching a dart here, a seam there. After studying the back of the dress for a while, he brings out a tape and starts taking measurements. Normally, I would be self-conscious, but Nelson is completely businesslike, so I relax.

"Got it," he says. "Now step up onto this stool and let me pin the hem." He makes a few marks using tailor's chalk, then picks up a box of straight pins and starts working his way around the stool on his hands and knees. Meanwhile, I stare at myself in the mirror. Again, there are three of me, from different angles, and somehow — it might be the dress or the way I've pulled all my hair up off my neck — I look like I'm somebody different. Older, maybe, and a little more worldly. A girl who might actually go to New York and walk down a red carpet.

I wonder what it'll be like. I think of the scene I saw from *Angel*, with the dance-hall girls wearing swirling long skirts like the one Nelson's pinning, and I start to imagine I'm one of them. Maybe the girl whose dance partner is Adam Kessler, the one he calls Angel. I feel like he's staring right into my eyes, his gaze deep as he whirls me around. My petticoats flare out and swirl, and morph into the wedding gown. Adam is leading me down a short aisle, like at the end of Act Two of *Our Town*, and Riley's reciting the vows, and I'm Emily Webb and Adam's George Gibbs and the Moment of Kiss is approaching.

My dad picks this moment to exit his office. "What are you doing?" he thunders when he catches sight of me in the wedding gown.

"I needed a model for this alteration," Nelson explains. "The bride's the same size as Diana. Her mother, who wore this dress first, was two sizes bigger."

Dad looks at my face in the mirror, and I see his expression grow softer. He reaches a hand toward mine and says quietly, "You look so much like her." I don't have to ask who he means. I can see it myself, from three different angles. Dad's eyes seem to shine in the lights.

"Don't grow up too fast," he says, turning away.

On Wednesday, Cat and I take our afternoon break in the ladies' room of Sam's Diner, which has a wall-to-wall mirror over the sinks. We have dubbed it the TRESemmé Hair Salon, just like on *Project Runway*. Cat's brought in her curling iron and a makeup case the size of a hatbox, and we're trying out red-carpet looks. We're hampered a bit by the fact that Nelson refuses to tell us a thing about what he's concocting, except to say, "Trust me, you will be *dazzling*." Cat has colored my left lid with three shades of eye shadow and is adding mascara when Elise bursts in, wild-eyed. "Mac attack!"

"Hide!" says Cat, grabbing her eye-shadow compacts. We skid into the Handicapped stall, barring the door and pressing ourselves to the far corner wall.

"Case!" I hiss loudly. Elise snaps the makeup case shut and slam-dunks it over the stall door, just as the door to the bathroom opens for Miss MacInerny.

"You're not supposed to leave the front counter until Catalina comes back from her break," she says. "Who's helping customers, Elise?"

"Sorry," Elise mumbles. "I'll go right back." She slinks out of the bathroom, leaving us to watch Miss MacInerny's feet go into a stall.

"That was soooooo close!" Cat laughs in the locker room after work.

"The best was you hiding the curling iron under your smock!"

"How about you, with your one-eye mascara?" We're both cracking up at our narrow escape, when I notice Elise isn't laughing. She's bent over her running shoes, tying them into tight knots.

"Thanks for letting us know MacInerny was coming," I tell her.

"Yeah, and for saving our butts with the makeup case," Cat chimes in.

Elise straightens up to her full five feet ten. "You two may enjoy taking chances and pushing your luck, but I'm not going to cover for you anymore."

"Sorry," says Cat.

"Me, too," I say, feeling about two feet tall.

Elise shrugs. "It's no biggie. Just take your own risks from now on, okay? I don't want to get fired."

I can't sleep that night. I keep staring up at the sloping wall over my bed, where all of my *Playbills* are on display. Where am I going to hide my *Angel* program (autographed by Adam Kessler, I hope)? Under the mattress? For the first time, I wish I was not going to see it this way. I've been painting it all as a giant adventure, but when you get down to it, I'm going to be lying to Dad and sneaking around — - taking chances, just like Elise said. It doesn't sit well in my stomach.

I've been thinking about Mom a whole lot today, ever since Dad made that comment about my resembling her. I remember her hand grasping mine at *The Lion King*, and then I picture her sitting with me at the *Angel* premiere, with the lights going down and the orchestra tuning. I remember the way she'd always lean over at the start of every show and whisper excitedly into my ear, "Magic time!"

Then I get an idea. I'll wear something that was hers, and that way she'll be with me, a little. I get out of bed and kneel down by the trunk where I've kept all her things, wrapped in tissue paper. The lingering scent of her perfume wafts up as I touch an old nightgown, a sweater I loved. Underneath those pieces is a blue velvet jewelry box that belonged to *her* mother. I know what's inside it: a few pairs of earrings, a hand-me-down silver and amethyst brooch, and a string of real pearls that Mom got as a graduation present and wore on her first date with Dad. Before she went into the hospital for her last chemo, she gave the pearls to me. It chilled me right to the bone. I knew she was trying to tell me she wouldn't be there for my graduation, or my first date with whoever I'd wind up marrying, and I didn't want to hear any such thing.

But now I feel ready to wear Mom's pearls to an opening night, just like she would have done. I open the box, and the necklace is gone.

I storm down the stairs to Ashley and Brynna's room, flipping the light switch on. I don't care if I wake them both up. "Where's my necklace?" I shout. "Did one of you take my pearl necklace?"

Brynna turns over in her bottom bunk, under her puffy purple quilt, her expression sleepy and confused. "What necklace?" she says.

I step onto the bunk ladder and grab Ashley's arm. "You took it, didn't you?"

"What are you talking about? You're insane," she snaps, twisting away. Her pink quilt slides off the top bunk, but I don't let her go.

"Give it back!"

"What makes you think I'd want anything that belonged to *you*?"

"It belonged to my *mother*," I hiss. "It isn't a dress-up toy!"

"Mo-om!" Ashley shouts. "Diana is hurting me!"

I can feel the tears stinging my eyes. "I want my pearl necklace."

The bedroom door bangs open and Fay strides in. "Let go of her this instant," she commands. I drop Ashley's wrist and step down off the bunk ladder, turning to face her. She's wearing a silver plush robe and pink slippers. She holds out one hand. In her palm is my mother's pearl necklace.

I grab it before she can speak, and storm out of the bedroom. As I rush blindly upstairs, I hear Fay tell the twins to go back to sleep.

Chapter Seven

I don't look at Fay once during breakfast. She doesn't exist in my world. Dad's reading the paper and sipping his decaf. Ashley's eating canned peaches, and Brynna is smearing her toast with Nutella. I clomp around in my boots, packing my school lunch — the twins will buy cafeteria pizza — and stuffing my books in my backpack. I'd like to take off without saying a word. But I know if I wait to ask Dad at the cleaners, he's going to defer the decision to that woman he married — I won't say her name — so I might as well spit it out now.

"Can I sleep over at Jess's tomorrow? It's opening night of the play, and there's a big party afterward."

"Sounds like fun," says Dad. "Fay?"

She looks at me for a long moment, then turns back to Dad. "We have plans with the Cunninghams."

"What plans?"

"The ballet in Newark, remember? That Junior League fund-raiser."

Dad groans. "Do we have to?"

"We do," Fay says firmly. "It's business. And I need Diana to sit for the twins."

"But it's opening night of *Our Town*!" I protest.

"I can stay with the girls," Dad says quickly.

Fay shakes her head. "You're coming with me. Nonnegotiable." Her eyes meet mine on the last word.

I'm venting to Jess as we head for our lockers. "She won't ever cut me a break. She goes out of her way to be mean to me!"

"Course she does." Jess's voice is matter-of-fact. "You're a living reminder your dad had a life before she came along. Must squash and conquer." Jess's parents are divorced and her dad is remarried, so she's wise in the ways of grown-up relationships.

"What am I going to do? I can't sit for those bratlets! I'm supposed to see *Angel*! And meet Adam Kessler!"

"Wish I could help, but I've got an opening night myself. Last night's dress rehearsal was a total fiasco, BTW. Thanks for asking."

I suddenly realize I skipped our phone call last night, for the first time in years. "*Rewind*," I say. Jess just looks at me, not playing along. "How did it go?"

She shrugs, her expression grim. "You know what they say: bad dress rehearsal, worse opening night."

"Isn't it 'bad dress, great opening'?"

"Not at Weehawken Middle School."

Will ambles past with his Sharpie-scrawled notebook just in time to overhear our exchange. Today's T-shirt says RADIOHEAD. "We'll pull it off, Jess, you'll see," he says.

"Dream on," she replies. Will's eyes slide over toward me, and he dips his chin, mumbling, "See you." This is kind of funny, since he just *did* see me — we were sitting together in English and he didn't say a word to me, just drew on his notebook.

Jess watches him walk away, nudging me. "What did I tell you?"

I roll my eyes, twisting open my locker. Adam's photo is smiling at me.

And then something occurs to me: Could Jess be so focused on Will because *she* has a crush on *him*? I sneak a peek in her direction, but her face gives away nothing. Besides, Jess is my best friend. She tells me her secrets and I tell her mine. Right?

As soon as I get to the cleaners, even before I put on my smock, I go into Dad's office and close the door. He looks up, surprised. "Are you having issues with Joy MacInerny again?"

No, Dad. I'm having issues with somebody worse. "It's not that. I really, really want to sleep over at Jess's tomorrow. It's bad enough I couldn't *be* in the play this year — can't I at least go to opening night?"

"Believe me, if I could stay home from that Newark ballet . . ."

"I could hire a sitter to stay with the twins. I've saved up some money."

Dad looks at me. "Honey, I've already talked to Fay about this. At length. It's not just about who can stay with the twins. She thinks I'm too lenient with you."

"Do you think she's right?" I fix him with a stare, and he sighs, leaning back in his desk chair.

"Fay had to bus tables at her family's restaurant when she was young, and when she wasn't working, she had to take care of her brothers and sisters. Nobody ever made any exceptions for her, and she thinks it builds character."

Oh, it does. "She took Mom's necklace!"

"She did not *take* it. She put it in safekeeping with her own valuables." I stare at him, realizing it's hopeless. How can he possibly take her side? Fay had no right to go through my things and no right not to tell me. I'm on the point of blurting this out when I notice a change in Dad's face.

"These aren't good times, honey. People are scared to spend money on things like fancy clothes and dry cleaning, and Fay's real estate sales are feeling the pinch. It's important for her to go out with her boss. It's important for *us*."

"Are we poor?"

"We are *not* poor. But we're struggling a little, like everyone else, and we all have to make sacrifices. Even of things that we love." He reaches across his desk, squeezing my hand. "I wish I could just tell you yes."

I nod and go back to the locker room, feeling so sad that it barely sinks in when Cat enters and tells me that Jared's van broke down this morning. So much for our ride to the city.

The day seems to drag on forever. Elise is preoccupied with a chemistry test, Cat and I are depressed, and even the clothes that people drop off seem grayer than usual. It's never occurred to me that Cinderella Cleaners might be struggling. It's been like a rock my whole life, the business my grandparents founded. And now they've retired to a senior center in Florida, and Dad's got to keep the whole place afloat by himself. Some of the people who work here — Loretta and Sadie, Rose and Mr. Chen — have practically spent their whole lives in these jobs. I know Dad would tell me the truth if the business was really in trouble, but suddenly things seem a lot more complex. I can see why he needs Fay, not just for the income her real estate business brings in, but for her no-nonsense, we'll-deal-with-it attitude. She keeps him on top.

And me on the bottom. That's just how it is.

The only person who's cheerful today is Nelson. Every time he sees me or Cat, he says something like, "Prepare to be stunned." I don't have the heart to tell him we can't even go. One more person to be disappointed. Maybe I should give Nelson the tickets, and he can design his own outfit for the red carpet.

Cat is not quite as discreet. "Nelson, you gotta stop saying this stuff, okay? We've got no ride and Diana's stuck playing nanny tomorrow."

"All will be well," Nelson crows as he hands me a pair of men's pants he's just hemmed, and though I think he's out of his mind, I appreciate his vote of confidence.

I'm taking the pants back to hang up with their jacket when, at the customer counter, I spot the last person on earth I was hoping to see.

Kayleigh Carell is inside Cinderella Cleaners, standing beside a blond woman who must be her mother. Kayleigh's wearing a white puffy jacket from Hollister over a lightwash denim miniskirt, white tights, and Uggs. She takes one look at me in my baggy smock, holding a pair of men's trousers, and her smile stretches wider. I want to sink through the floor.

"Di-aaan-ah!" she says, running my name up and down the scale. "Is it a small world, or what?"

Or what, I think sourly. Kayleigh knows perfectly well where I work after school, and I can't help thinking she brought her opening-night dress to be dry-cleaned just so she could gloat. The unwritten laws of middle school social life keep me from saying so, though. I pull my face into a pleasant expression and say, "Really. Wow."

"The play's going great," she says. "I am *sooo* nervous."

This is a clear piece of bait, planted so I'll reassure her she's going to be fabulous. "Just remember to breathe," I say, hoping she doesn't.

Kayleigh smiles. "Are you coming on opening night?"

"I wish," I tell her. "But I have to babysit Friday."

"Oh, too bad," Kayleigh says, puffing her lower lip out in a little fake pout. Her eyes land on my name tag, and I can just tell that she's going to describe every detail to Zane. Not to mention her best friend, Savannah.

Elise hands Kayleigh's mother the customer copy of her receipt, and Kayleigh trills, "Bye-bye!"

As soon as they leave, Nelson taps me on the shoulder. "Let me tell you something about middle school. The girls on the top of the heap? It's all downhill from there. This is the absolute peak of their lives, but the people they pick on, they're just getting started. You hear what I'm telling you?"

"Thanks," I say glumly.

"You hear me, but you don't believe me," says Nelson. "That girl who just left, she'll be serving you donuts some-day." He goes back to the Tailoring section.

Elise looks at me sympathetically. "'Someday' doesn't help much with right now, does it?"

"Not much," I say, staring at Kayleigh's dress.

At the end of the workday, Nelson tells me and Cat to stay after hours for a fitting. "Tell your dad you'll be getting a ride home with Cat, and then hide in the locker room closet," he says, and I realize he must have hidden in the men's room broom closet the night I caught him on a bor-rowing mission.

There's only one problem: The women's room closet is tiny. Cat might be able to squeeze in there next to the Lysol and paper supplies, but there's no way we'll both fit. The toilet stall door is too high — you'd see way too much leg underneath, and anyway, somebody might have to use the bathroom before she heads home. I don't want to give Sadie a heart attack.

Nelson solves this problem, too. "Hide in the dressing room," he tells me. "The curtain goes all the way down to the floor." So as soon as Loretta and Sadie straighten up from their sewing machines and head back to the locker room, grumbling and lurching on weary feet, Cat distracts MacInerny with some scheduling question, and I scuttle into the dressing room, pulling the curtain closed slowly and carefully so it won't make noise.

After a beat, I hear Cat say, "Okay, thanks. Bye, Mr. Donato!" The swinging doors open and close, and there's nobody left in the front but my father and Miss MacInerny. I hear the cash register bell, the sound of a cash drawer being removed, and the rustling of paper as someone counts bills.

"It's short twenty dollars." MacInerny's tone is accusatory. "Again."

"Are you sure?" Dad asks.

"It's the third time this month."

"I'm sure it's just human error. The cash drawer was *over* once, too."

"Once," MacInerny says. "That's the smart thing to do when you're stealing: Make it look like a mistake. It's one of those high school girls, I'm sure of it."

It's all I can do not to yell at the top of my lungs. How could she possibly think Cat or Elise would steal money from Dad? I clench and unclench my fists, making myself take deep breaths and stay still.

Dad sighs and says, "I don't see any hard evidence. And I'm not about to accuse anybody unless I do."

Way to go, Dad!

I'm so angry at MacInerny, I feel like I'm going to explode. I stand in the dressing room, imagining various ways to torment her, until I hear her say good night and go out the front door, heels clicking sharply.

Dad sighs as he zips the cash into a bank deposit bag. I

hear him walk toward the door with heavy footsteps, pausing to switch off the overhead lights and turn on the burglar alarm. From outside, I hear him fumbling to lock the front door with his heavy key ring. His footsteps recede.

I make myself wait till I hear a car start and pull out, and then I burst out of the dressing room and run through the double doors.

Oh, no! I forgot all about the dark workroom! I'm so angry I'm practically not even scared. I'm not careful enough, either: I send a laundry cart rolling across the floor and then bump right into a worktable corner, yelling "Ow!" without thinking. The overhead lights switch on full, and I gasp. But it's only Nelson, banging open the door to the men's locker room.

"Let's start the show," he intones, snapping on the workroom boom box. Techno music echoes off the cleaning machines. Cat steps out of the locker room, striking a pose. She's swathed in a deep orange satin gown that looks great with her dark eyes and hair. It has double spaghetti straps and a flattering neckline. The hemline is flirty, with an asymmetrical flounce that adds length to her legs.

As the music pounds, Cat does her best runway walk in high heels, throwing her shoulders back and swinging her hips. At the pressing machine, she stops, strikes another pose, turns, and walks back. The dress seems to dance by itself.

Nelson whistles and claps, yelling, "Work it!" I join the applause, and Cat's high-fashion pout dissolves into her usual grin.

"I totally love it!" she says, hugging Nelson. "Wait till you see it with my gold hoop earrings and my hair done. I'm so gonna sizzle!"

Before I can remind her we're not going anywhere, Nelson throws open the broom closet's door. The words freeze in my mouth. Hanging there on the back of the door is The Dress's first cousin, in textured white satin with black lace trim. It's adorable.

"Where did you get it?" I gasp.

"Get it? I *made* it!" Nelson sounds mortally wounded.

I shake my head. "I meant the fabric. It's gorgeous!"

Nelson smiles. "Remember the train on that bridal gown, and the black satin blouse on the No Pickup rack? *Voila!*"

I take a step forward and run my hand over the fabric. It's glossy and elegant, and I picture my pearl necklace framed in the neckline. I know the dress will fit me like a glove, and I can't wait to wear it to *Angel*.

We've *got* to find some way to get there!

Chapter Eight

It's finally Friday. I wish I could press the FAST FORWARD button through my science quiz, through health class, and a history unit on Civil War battles (again!). The worst is having to sit through an oral report by Kayleigh Carell, who's doing this phony movie-star thing of "protecting her voice" by wrapping her throat with a scarf and speaking in an overdone breathy whisper.

Even lunch is a drag. Jess is falling apart with opening-night jitters. She can't even look at her food, and keeps asking me if she'll be all right. "What if I throw up backstage?" she says.

"I promise you won't."

"I'm already nauseous."

"You will *not* throw up," I tell her. I'm on autopilot. All I can think of is how I can make it to *Angel* — tonight! My mind swarms with getaway plots but keeps hitting a brick wall named Fay.

Sara and Amelia sit down at our table. All day long, I've been asking my friends if they're free for a last-minute babysitting job — I said I'd pay double! — but everyone's either involved with *Our Town* or has other plans. Amelia already told me in gym that her family is going away for the weekend, but I haven't seen Sara all day. Maybe, just maybe, she'll bail me out.

I watch as she unzips her lunch bag, revealing two take-out containers from her family's Indian restaurant. The food smells delicious, as always. "Have you got any plans for tonight?" I ask Sara as she takes off lids.

"We're catering somebody's wedding rehearsal. I have to bus tables. Who wants a samosa?"

"I can't eat a thing," moans Jess.

"Great," says Amelia, reaching for one. "You want some of my coleslaw?"

I shake my head. *Everyone's* busy tonight. It's totally, utterly hopeless. Not even Nelson Martinez can fix this.

• • •

Elise works at the cash register, handing change to a regular customer. I notice the way MacInerny is eyeballing her every move, and as soon as we get a free moment together, I tell her what I overheard yesterday. Elise gets so freaked out, I almost think she might be guilty of something, but then I remember how worried she is about ever getting in trouble. When I tell Cat, her reaction is much more like mine.

"I'll kill her," she says. "I will murder her dead."

"I'll help."

"How could she think I would do that?"

"She never said it was *you*."

"Yeah, but look who she's got at the counter: Miss Seven-foot Perfect. She's got *me* stashed away in the back, where I can't get my hands in the cash drawer."

This gives me an idea.

The next time I go to the bathroom, I stop at my locker and dig through my wallet, tucking the twenty-dollar bill I always keep for an emergency into my pocket. Every time I go up to the customer counter, I look for my moment.

Finally it comes. Elise has opened the register drawer, and she turns away, grabbing a handful of bags from the conveyor belt to hand to her customer. I sidle right past the register, dropping my bill in the drawer.

Elise might have noticed me passing the counter, but I'm positive she didn't catch my smooth move, since my back blocked her view of my hand. My logic is simple: If today's total shows twenty dollars too much, MacInerny will have to accept that yesterday's shortfall was just because of a mislaid bill. I'm feeling extremely smug and generous about using my money to help someone else, but when I turn around with the laundry cart, Elise hands back my twenty.

"You put it in with the fives," she says. "I don't steal. So you don't have to cover for me."

Her expression is fierce, and I feel like an idiot. "I know you don't steal," I stammer. "I was just trying to help. I know how much you need this job to do basketball camp."

Elise's face softens. "I know that you meant well, Diana," she says. "But you could have gotten us both in a mess. What if MacInerny saw you with your hand in the

106

till? She'd think *you* were stealing. Promise you won't ever do that again."

"I won't," I say, chastened.

"But thanks for the thought." She gives me a little fist bump on the arm, and I feel better.

The rest of the day stumbles on, with Nelson making comments about opening night and red carpets whenever he sees me. I keep telling Cat she should bring Jared to opening night in my place. If his van's still not running, they're old enough to go on the PATH train. "Even if he *hates* Broadway musicals, you'll get to go to a big catered dance party afterward. And you can't tell me he won't enjoy seeing you in that dress."

"Jared's not going to go for it, trust me."

"Then you go with Nelson."

Cat snorts. "Yeah, that'll play great with my jealous jock boyfriend. Seeing me get in a car in a bright orange dress with some cute Latin guy. Good one, Diana."

I hadn't thought of that. Nelson's twenty-three, enough older than Cat that I can't really see him as datable, and besides that, he's *Nelson*.

"That ticket is *yours*," Cat says. "You're the one who found it, you're the one who's crazy about Broadway shows, you're the one who's gonna go."

She's right about two out of three at least.

At the end of the workday, when we're changing out of our smocks, my heart is as heavy as it's ever been. The opening of *Angel* is only a few hours away, and I'm not going to be there. Two orchestra tickets, fifth row on the aisle, and they're just going to go to waste. It's a crime against nature.

Sadie and Loretta pull on their coats, both talking at once about what they're making for dinner ("I'll just heat it up in the microwave Gloria brought me"). As soon as they leave the room ("My matzo balls are like *feathers*"), Cat reaches into her locker and takes out a pair of glittery stiletto heels.

"Ta-da!"

"What are those?"

"For you. Can't go to an opening night in a ball gown and Converse."

What is she not getting? "I've told you a hundred times, Cat, I can't go at all!"

"That's what you think." She puts a shoe on each hand and walks them down the bench, *tap tap tap*.

"But I don't have a sitter! You think I'm just going to leave Ashley and Brynna at home by themselves? I'm not *that* irresponsible!"

Elise, who's been bent over lacing her running shoes, stands up and grabs her pink hoodie. "As a matter of fact, I'm a *great* babysitter."

I stare at her, my jaw dropping. "You would *do* that for me?"

"Why not?" says Elise. "I've got the night free and my parents said they'll let me borrow the car. What time do you need me to be there?"

"Oh, my god!" I leap off the bench and start whooping and hugging her. So does Cat. I hear the two shoes clatter down to the floor, but I don't even care.

"I don't believe this! Thank you so, so, *so* much!" We're both hugging Elise at the same time, and she shakes us off, tossing her hair.

"You two are both nuts."

"Yeah, but you love us," says Cat, and Elise cracks a smile.

I'm so happy I feel like singing. Sometimes I wish life was a musical.

The hard part is making myself look the way I would actually feel if I had to stay home with the twins, when in reality I'm so incredibly happy. As Dad drives me home, I keep my arms folded and stare out the window. It's a real acting challenge to pout and look mad when I'm on my way to see *Angel*. I should get an Oscar for this performance. At one point, Dad glances at me and again says, "I wish . . ."

You don't have to wish anything, I want to tell him. *My dream's coming true.*

As soon as we're home, I stride angrily past Fay — no acting required — and slam up to my room, where I put on loud music to "make myself feel better." Actually, so I can place a phone call to Jess from within stepmother radar.

"I'm going!" I whisper into my phone as Pink blasts through my bedroom.

"To *Our Town*?"

"To *Angel*!"

Jess lets out a scream so loud I'm afraid Fay will hear it right through the door. "I don't believe this! You lucky stiff! Who's going to stay with —"

"Elise. I'll be back really late, and I have to change outfits before I go home. Can I still come over?"

"Of course! And my mom is on night shift. She can't see *Our Town* till next week."

Perfect! "What about your brother?"

There's an odd pause. "He's in the play."

"What? Since when?"

"Another sixth grader dropped out and Dash took over his part. He's playing one of the baseball players, big stretch. I told you last week."

Now I feel really bad for not paying attention. "I guess I've been kind of preoccupied."

"Kind of." Jess's voice is sarcastic, but I know her so well I can tell she's more nervous than mad at me.

"You're going to be great in the play, Jess. And I can't wait to hear all about it, so break a linguini."

"Yeah? Break a Liberty Bell. Again."

"Good one!" I roll out my best Beatles accent. "Break a Liverpool, luv."

"See you later tonight," Jess laughs. "Tell Adam Kessler to break a lip."

Fay takes *forever* to put on her outfit. It's hard to say why, since she looks the same as she always looks, like somebody cut her suit out of the office furniture fabric by accident. She's wearing silver shell earrings and so much hair spray that she seems to be wearing an ash-blond bike helmet. Dad's in his usual suit and a tie that Fay gave him last Christmas.

"How late will you be?" I ask, carefully keeping my sulk in place.

Dad looks at Fay, who's regarding me with unguarded suspicion, as if she's convinced that I'm going to pull something. "I don't know. We'll be going for drinks with the Cunninghams after the ballet," she says, weighing her words. "We'll be sure to check in with you."

Gulp.

Ashley and Brynna follow them out to the SUV. We stand on the front lawn, waving as they back out of the driveway and pull away, honking a hasty good-bye. My eyes are across the street, where a silver hatchback and a green van are waiting.

Ashley turns to me with a satisfied smirk. "So you're stuck with us after all."

"That's what you think," I tell her, as Elise pops open the hatchback and starts taking things out. "You just got a new babysitter."

"What?" Brynna cringes.

Ashley is furious. "You heard what Mom said! We are so going to tell on you."

"Why would you want to do that?" says Elise, stepping up with an armload of DVDs, candy boxes, and two tubs of popcorn. A shopping bag dangles from her other arm. "My name is Elise, and we're going to have a great time."

Brynna's eyes are enormous, and even Ashley says, "What'd you get?"

"All kinds of cool stuff," says Elise, handing over the tower of movies so the twins can paw through it. "You guys like Harry Potter? *High School Musical?* Disney?"

"Whoa! This is not even *out* yet," Ashley says, holding up some DVD box in glittery pink.

Elise shrugs and smiles. "It is now. I brought art supplies, too, and a bunch of video games."

I'm in awe. Elise grins at me. "Didn't I ever tell you my dad runs a video store? Get going — you're going to be late."

"Where are you going?" Brynna demands, turning toward me.

"A play," says Elise, her voice reassuring. "She'll be back soon. So who do you like the best, Harry or Ron or Hermione?"

"Thanks a billion," I say, scooting across the street and into the van, where Cat is waiting.

"Wow, I thought your Dad and stepmom would never leave," says Cat. "Hope this thing starts." She twists the ignition key and the van rattles to life.

"What was wrong with it?" I yell over the din.

"Muffler!" she yells back. I look over my shoulder and see Elise leading Ashley and Brynna back into the house. The twins look as happy as clams.

We are running late. Nelson has set up a dressing room for us in the back rooms of Cinderella Cleaners, but first we run into the Sam's Diner TRESemmé Hair Salon to fix our faces. Cat puts on a bit too much mascara and blush. At one point a customer comes in and gawks at us.

"How come you girls are dressed up so fancy?" she rasps in a deep cigarette croak.

"Quinceañera party," says Cat at the same time that I say, "Cousin's wedding."

She stares at us blankly. "Whatever."

It feels a bit strange to run across the parking lot in jeans, a half-zipped hoodie, hot-curled hairdo, and makeup. Nelson's left the employee entrance propped open for us and we pile through the door, laughing breathlessly as we pass the HAVE YOU SWIPED TODAY? sign. Our gowns are hung up on the door of the ladies' locker room, and as soon as we've zipped ourselves in, Nelson comes to make final adjustments, checking the alterations he did on Cat's bodice and rearranging the drape of my skirt. He looks at me, stepping backward and frowning.

"You need to lose a few layers of makeup. You look like you're going to Amy Winehouse's sweet sixteen."

"Thanks a lot!" says Cat.

"Diana's got delicate features," he says. "You don't

want to drown her in eyeliner. Lighten that blush while you're at it."

Cat dabs at my face with a towelette, toning things down. She applies a fresh brushing of neutral face powder.

"Better?" she asks.

Nelson nods. "But you need something here, at the throat."

"Oh!" I exclaim, digging in my jeans pocket. I take out a striped sock and he raises his eyebrows. I stick my fingers into the toe and pull out Mom's pearl necklace.

"Perfect!" he says as I reach my arms back to fix the clasp. "And the shoes?"

"Got 'em," says Cat, pulling out the stilettos.

"*Dios mio*," says Nelson. "The child has to *walk*."

"Yeah, but her foot's a size bigger than mine. They were all I could find with an open back. They're by Baby Phat."

Nelson sets the shoes down on the floor and I step into them, wobbling a bit on the tapering heels.

Cat whistles. "Look at you, girl! You're as tall as Elise!" She's strapping on her own shoes, black patent with slightly flared heels.

"Just don't twist your ankle," says Nelson. He hands me a small velvet evening bag. "Put your tickets in here. Nobody carries a backpack with Nelson Couture."

I transfer my tickets, wallet, and cell phone into the hand-sewn bag and stand up straight, feeling my posture elongate. Nelson scoops up our cast-off clothes, holding my Converse at fingertip length as if they were twin skunks.

"Now come out and look at yourself." He throws open the door to the hall, where he's set up the three-way mirror from Tailoring, right where an overhead light angles down like a spotlight. I see myself coming and gasp.

Who is that elegant girl? I can't see that reflection as me: She looks stunning, grown up, like a different person. The black-and-white gown complements my dark hair, and the pearl necklace gleams at my throat. When did I grow those cheekbones, those collarbones? And I'm so *tall*.

"Well?" Nelson says with a satisfied smirk. "Are you gorgeous?"

Behind him, Cat bursts into applause. "Encore! Encore!"

I see her reflection join mine in the mirror, wearing her bright orange dress. Her bare shoulders are draped in a black satin shawl, shot through with glittering threads that echo the sheen of her black patent pumps.

"Wow! You look fabulous!"

"Takes one to know one," says Cat.

"Takes one to *dress* one," says Nelson.

"You are the best, *mi amor*," Cat exclaims. She kisses his cheek, which is all she can reach. I'm too embarrassed to give Nelson an actual kiss, but I give him a quick hug and pat on the back.

"Thank you so much. They're amazing."

Cat looks at us both in the mirror. "Can you believe we'll be wearing these clothes in a secondhand van?"

Nelson's eyes twinkle. "Step outside."

"Huh?" says Cat.

"Just do it."

We head down the hall, Cat in confident strides and me wobbling a little on my stilettos. Nelson opens the door, and a breath of cool night air flows in. Then we see it.

"Oh . . . my . . . GOD!!!"

Cat and I scream at the same time. A white stretch limo is heading our way from its hiding place on the far side of the building.

Cat and I start gushing, our words overlapping. "I don't believe this! Where did it come from? Wow!!!"

The limo pulls up at the door, and the driver rolls down his window. He's an older man with sparkling eyes and a spotless black uniform.

"Meet my uncle Mark," Nelson says. He leans toward the window and hands his uncle a shopping bag full of our clothes.

"For later," he says. "And I owe you one."

Mark shrugs. "*De nada.* You'll fix me a suit jacket someday."

Nelson holds open the long middle door, revealing a wraparound banquette with leather upholstery, a wide-screen TV, and a mini-fridge. Cat and I hold hands and jump up and down, shrieking like fans at a pop concert.

Nelson turns back to Mark. "I promise they won't stay this squeaky."

"No problem," says Mark. "I've seen worse. Try Jersey City on prom night."

Cat and I climb into the back of the limo, gasping with awe. It's as big as a room. The seats are as soft as down comforters, and the windows are lined with rows of lights like constellations.

Nelson gives us a wave. "Have a ball," he grins as he pulls the door shut, ignoring our chorus of thank-yous. The limo pulls forward and we're on our way.

This is already the very best night of my life.

Chapter Nine

My favorite view is all dressed up for evening. The night-lit skyscrapers sparkle like jewels on a black satin sky. By some miracle, traffic is light on the spiral ramp down to the Lincoln Tunnel. As we swoop down the fast lane, passing a long row of cars, I watch people's heads swivel to look at our limo, wondering, as I always do, "Who's in *there*?"

We are, I want to shout out. *Diana Donato and Catalina James, VIPs!*

Cat knocks on the partition, and Mark rolls it down.

"Is it okay to use this stuff?" she asks.

"Not the fridge, please. I've got to pick up my real client as soon as I drop you off. Don't want any loose Coke cans or chips on the seats."

"Got it," says Cat. "But I meant the TV."

"Sure, be my guest," says Mark. Cat grabs the remote and takes aim. This reminds me of something. I speed-dial my home number.

Elise picks up on the third ring. "Donato residence."

"Don't say that," I tell her. "Fay might call to check on me."

"*What?*"

"Just pick up with 'hello' and use really short words. 'Fine.' 'Uh-huh.' 'Bye.'"

"I'm not going to lie."

"You won't have to. I never say much when I'm mad, so they'll think you're me. If push comes to shove, tell them I went to opening night. Just don't say which one."

"Your father's my boss, you know."

"I swear you won't get in trouble. It's me they'll be mad at." They really will, too, but that can't be helped. This is worth anything.

Just then, Cat grabs my hand, pulling the phone toward her mouth. "We're in a stretch limo!" she shouts. "It's got wide-screen TV!"

"Don't gloat," says Elise, a bit sourly. "I'm watching an Olsen twins marathon."

"You get a gold medal," I tell her as our limo pulls out of the tollbooth lane and enters the mouth of the tunnel.

The Lincoln Tunnel always gives me a shiver of anticipation. The yellowish sheen of the tiles and the amber lights streaking past make it feel like a time-travel special effect in a sci-fi movie. As we burrow deep underground, the TV signal flickers to static.

"Won't get much reception down here. There's a few billion gallons of water between you and the signal," says Mark. "But there's lots of CDs back there."

"Cool!" breathes Cat. She's like a kid in a candy store, bouncing in her leather seat, peering into the mini-fridge, sampling the stereo speakers. I'd rather just stare out the window and feel the excitement building inside of me, as we get closer and closer to Broadway. I can already sense that the tunnel is sloping back upward. We're almost there!

I love where the Lincoln Tunnel comes out: on the long block of 42nd Street called Theatre Row. The first thing we see is marquees for shows, lit up in bright colors. Everything looks alive. The sidewalks are overflowing with people from thousands of places in thousands of outfits:

black leather jackets and shimmery saris and tailored suits. A man in a turban shouts into his cell as he passes a woman in a striped sweater dress, walking a dog in a tartan plaid coat. There are lights and sounds coming from every direction, the energy crackling like fireworks. When our limo pulls into Times Square, with its megawatt billboards and blinking lights, I want to give it a standing ovation.

"Listen up, ladies," says Mark. "Nelson tells me you're going to the after-show gala. Your pickup is midnight sharp, outside the restaurant. I need to shuttle a client around town for a couple of hours, but he's tied up from midnight till one. That's my window. If you're late, I can't wait for you. You'll have to pay for a cab back to Jersey. Got that?"

"We'll be on the dot." I nod.

"Who are you driving?" asks Cat. "Somebody famous?"

"More famous than you can imagine," Mark deadpans. He turns onto a side street and pulls up in front of the theatre, double-parking next to another stretch limo. There's a hubbub outside. Well-dressed theatergoers cluster under the marquee, near an area set up with powerful spotlights on poles and a TV truck. A video cameraman points his lens at a blond entertainment reporter who's swooping toward somebody stepping away from a third limo. Cat stretches across my lap to see who it is.

"Oh, my god, it's Sarah Jessica Parker. I *love* her!"

I can't believe my eyes. There are actual stars here. With us!

Mark puts on his uniform cap and leans over the seat. "Ready?"

"You bet!"

"Okay, you celebutantes. Here we go."

He steps out of the driver's seat and walks around to the side of the limo, holding the door open for us. "Slow and graceful," he winks with his back to the crowd. "You might be on camera."

Cat gasps, nervously touching a hand to her hair as I scramble back into my shoes. "All the time in the world," Mark intones reassuringly. "This is your moment."

"You first," I hiss at Cat.

"*You*," she insists.

I don't want to argue. I swing a leg out to the street, take Mark's outstretched hand, and straighten up. I can feel my heart pumping so hard I think everyone on the street must be able to hear it. My face is as warm as if I've run a race. Flashbulbs are popping, and I see a couple of teenage girls holding their cell phones high over their heads to snap photos of Sarah Jessica Parker. She's a model of cool, smiling for the crowd as the blond reporter asks, "Who are you wearing?"

"Jasmine Cee," Parker says, making a little half swirl to display her gown's Grecian draping. I can actually feel my palms sweating as I clutch my bag. I'm glad that the spotlights are trained on somebody else. This is a bit overwhelming.

I take an uneasy step toward the bright lights as Cat comes up behind me. She's pulled her shawl dramatically high, so her face is part hidden. "Maybe they'll think I'm America Ferrera," she whispers. "You be Anne Hathaway."

I don't have a shawl, so the best I can do is to shield my eyes from the bright lights with one hand as we make our way forward. People crane toward us, wondering who we are. The teen girls with the cell phones lean over the red velvet ropes to snap photos of us, just in case, and even the TV crew turns to take notice.

I keep my head high, trying to look glamorous and a little mysterious while my stomach lurches with nervous excitement. Is this what it feels like to be a real star? As we head down the cordon, a little redheaded girl standing next to her parents asks for my autograph. I'm utterly charmed.

"Of course," I say, taking the program and pen she holds out. "What's your name?"

"Ruby."

I write, "To Ruby, Dreams do come true!" and scrawl my name right next to Sarah Jessica Parker's. As I hand back the signed program and pen, she tells me solemnly, "I like your dress."

"Thank you," I beam, and Cat gushes, "It's Nelson Couture!"

The air in the lobby is thick with the smells of many different perfumes. Two ticket takers, a man and a woman with seen-it-all looks on their faces, stand in front of the door, tearing tickets. I dig in my purse and hand ours over, feeling a surge of joy as we enter the theatre.

An usher in one of those old-fashioned uniforms, black jacket with a circular white collar, shines her small flashlight on our ticket stubs. Instead of directing us right or left and up two flights of stairs to the rear mezzanine, like I'm used to, she dips her head, leading us straight ahead into the orchestra section. Am I imagining it, or does she see us differently: not just as two girls who like going to plays, but as people with clout who scored VIP tickets for opening night?

We follow her down the long aisle. Cat's gaping up at the ceiling, with its murals surrounded by flounces of gold. She's so awestruck, I'm sure she'll bump right into someone.

Our seats are thrillingly close to the stage, fifth row on the center aisle. The usher points them out, hands us two *Playbills*, and disappears.

"Here?" Cat says, eyes wide. "For real?"

"For real," I say, though I can hardly believe it myself. Cat goes in first, and I take the seat on the aisle. The seat next to Cat's is empty, and audience members are still settling into their places. A tuxedoed man in the third row stands backward in front of his seat, scowling impatiently and scanning the aisle for someone who must be running late. I see several more people I think may be famous. Is that guy in the corner Clay Aiken? I'm tempted to ask him to sing a few bars of "On My Way Here" to find out for sure. And could that be Tyra Banks two rows down the aisle? I can't see her whole face, but it looks like her profile.

I whisper to Cat and she follows my gaze.

"Oh my god, *yes*. It's totally her! This is so amazing!"

I have to agree. I still can't believe that we're actually *here*. And this is even before I've seen Adam Kessler onstage! I open my *Playbill* and flip through till I find the cast photos. There he is. I sigh. Even in black-and-white, his eyes are blue. I study his bio, though I've already read all his credits online. I try reading about other actors, like Sigrid Wilner, the girl who plays Angel. Sigrid's bio is so long, she must be much older than Adam, but I'm too excited to read much more.

Trying to calm myself down, I take a deep breath and stare at the curtain. It's a heavy brocade, and I'm glad it's pulled closed. Sometimes the curtain is already parted so you can look at the scenery, which is fun: You can pore over details and try to imagine what's going to happen in this room in the next two hours. But I like being surprised when the lights go out and the curtain comes up on a different world.

Cat has stopped staring at Tyra Banks, for now. She's lost in her *Playbill*, flipping through perfume ads. I lean forward to peer at the orchestra pit, which is lit from below. We can't see that much of the pit from our seats — just the top of a harp and the long scrolled neck of a stand-up bass — but I can make out the sounds of a flute running up the scale, somebody brushing a snare drum, an electric guitar player tuning his strings. I'm sitting like that when a deep voice says, "Marion?"

I nearly jump out of my skin. *Oh, no.*

It never occurred to me that the fur coat owner, Marion Lavin, might have bought seats next to someone she knew!

I turn toward the voice, trying my best not to shake. It's a silver-haired man in a Burberry trench coat and tortoise-shell glasses, and I'm just about to squeak out that we must be in the wrong seats (and *then* what?) when he breaks into a warm, friendly smile.

"Is that Cindy? Goodness, how lovely you look!" My eyes must be bugging out of my head, because he says kindly, "You don't remember me, do you? Miles Kessler. We met at your aunt's in the Hamptons last summer."

Miles . . . did he say *Kessler*? OMG! Not only does he think he's met me already, he must be related to Adam! Miles holds out his hand and I reach a limp hand up to shake it, so overwhelmed that all I can think of to say is, "Oh, yes."

My mind revs into overdrive. Aunt. He just said aunt. That means this Cindy person is Marion Lavin's niece, and she's been to the Hamptons. I need more to go on. There's this improvisation exercise I did in drama club once where one partner has all the facts and the other has to figure out who they are without asking questions. I'm racking my brain to remember the rules when Miles Kessler hands me a huge clue. "How's your exchange program going? New York must feel awfully different from London."

London? Yikes, accent! I hope I can summon mine from *My Fair Lady*.

"It is, rather, yes." That could pass, I think. What did I say before, when he mentioned the Hamptons? "Oh, yes."

Fairly neutral for accent. I hope. It's a good thing I didn't say anything else.

"May I?" Miles gestures ahead with his program, indicating that he'd like to get to his seat, next to Cat's.

"So sorry." I scramble up to my feet, letting the folding seat flip up so he can get past. He looks startled by my height.

"Gracious, you've really grown up! I wasn't quite sure it was you, with your hair up like that, and . . ." And what? Different face, voice, and body?

"I'm not really this tall," I say hastily. "I expect it's the shoes. They belong to my fri . . . my chum, Catalina."

I gesture toward Cat, who's wedged into her seat, with an expression of frozen terror. Miles reaches to shake her hand, too. "Hello, Catalina. Miles Kessler."

She squeaks out a petrified "Hi." I gesture at her to let Miles pass by, and she presses herself back as if she'd like to disappear into her seat. There's no way she's going to be able to improvise dialogue, I realize as he sidles past us, shrugs out of his trench coat, and takes his seat. What if he starts asking her questions?

Inspiration strikes. "Catalina and I met in the exchange program," I report in my best London accent, while she stares at me like I've gone out of my mind. "She's from Guatemala."

Cat gets it. *"Si!"* she says gratefully, nodding and smiling as if she's embarrassed by how bad her English is. "From Quetzaltenango." This is her mother's hometown, so her accent's pitch-perfect. Solved *that* problem.

"Well, I'm delighted you girls could use Jeffrey and Marion's tickets," Miles says. "She was absolutely beside herself when her flight back was canceled."

I nod sympathetically. "I know," I say, though of course I *don't* know. Was Marion planning to fly back from Dubai just for opening night? How rich *is* this lady? And how well does she know this Miles Kessler?

Or Adam?

These mysteries will have to wait, though, because — not an instant too soon — the house lights are dimming. Cat looks up at the crystal chandelier. I lean forward, holding my breath as the audience settles down in a collective hush.

Magic time.

Chapter Ten

Angel is way beyond my wildest dreams. From the opening chords of the overture, my attention is glued to the stage.

The curtain comes up very fast, on an empty street in the Wild West. Somehow, they've made it look endless, as if a stray sagebrush that blew down this Main Street would roll way off into the desert, and not to a back wall on Broadway and 49th. No sooner is this ghostly image etched into our brains than a saloonkeeper in an apron comes to his window, lighting a gaslight. As it flares up, the stage rotates, which brings us inside the saloon bursting with color and life. And then the lead characters enter.

Three brothers running from the law. Are they desperadoes or good guys whose luck turned bad? The youngest one pulls off his Stetson hat and the dusty bandanna that's hiding his face, and my heart does a flip. It's *him*.

Cat blurts out, "*Cute*," then looks anxiously over at Miles to see if he noticed her English. He's grinning with pride, his eyes glued to the stage.

Adam's character, Cody Downs, staggers a little and grabs the back of a chair. His two brothers sit him down at a table. One goes to get water. The other rolls back Cody's shirtsleeve and examines his arm. He's been shot. We're ten minutes into the story and my heart is already pounding.

The show is over-the-top romantic, a tale of doomed love with a supercharged rock and roll sound track. The dancers throw off so much energy that Cat can barely sit still in her seat. But the high point for me is when Cody Downs sings a tender ballad to the sad-eyed young waitress that he's nicknamed Angel. How is it possible that he's holding her in his arms, looking right into her eyes, and seems to be singing directly to *me*?

When the lights come up for intermission, I don't want the spell to break. I want to stay in this moment forever, imagining I'm Cody's Angel. I'm still holding my breath as people around us start getting up from their seats. Miles Kessler turns toward me and Cat, and says, "So? What do you think of my grandson?"

Never have I had to improvise less. All I need to work on is keeping my London accent intact as I bubble and gush about Adam's acting, his beautiful voice, the way he dances. Cat nods her head, interjecting that he's *muy guapo*. From the look in her eye, I would guess this means "hottie."

Miles beams at us both. "Would you like to meet him?"

"What?" My accent just fell in the ocean, but Miles hasn't noticed.

"I'm going backstage to his dressing room afterward. I thought you might —"

"YES." I say this so loudly, the lady in front of me turns to stare. The couple on Miles's left have gotten to their feet and are waiting for him to stand up so they can pass by him. He says, "Shall we go stretch our legs?" and before I can think straight, we're walking up the aisle to the lobby, past a kiosk selling T-shirts and mugs, and a snack bar with coffee and overpriced chocolates. Cat gazes wistfully at the Toblerone bars.

The bald man ahead of us is barking at some maitre d' on his cell phone, and Miles reaches for his, flipping it open. "Let's call Marion at her hotel!" he exclaims. "You can tell her we've met!"

Cat turns pale and I feel my pulse go into hyperdrive. I don't have a clue how to keep him from dialing. In a total panic, I lurch forward, pretending that someone's bumped into me from behind, and knock the cell phone right out of his hand. It skids onto the carpet and I "catch my balance" by landing on top of it, hard, with the heel of Cat's shoe. I hear the display screen crack like a walnut.

"Oh, no!" I say, thinking, *Yes! Score!* "How dreadfully clumsy of me. Is it broken?"

Miles bends to retrieve it. He presses a button, but nothing lights up. "Don't worry about it," he says graciously. "High time for an upgrade. Would you like a drink or some candy?"

"We couldn't possibly," I say before Cat can beg for a Toblerone. "You're terribly kind, but I must find the ladies' loo."

"*Si,* me too also." Cat nods, and we scurry away toward the stairs.

As soon as we're out of earshot, Cat grabs my arm. "That was *awesome*!"

"You, too! 'Me too also,' with that little accent? See, you're getting into this. Next thing you know, you're going to be acting. You can play J.Lo's kid sister."

"You think?" she says, cracking up.

"I can't believe I stomped Adam Kessler's grandfather's cell phone."

"Don't sweat it. He looks plenty rich," Cat says, grinning. "And isn't it cool that we're going backstage?"

"I can't *wait*," I tell her, and that is the truth. We get onto the ladies' room line, which is three times as long as the men's. For the first time all evening, I think of the opening night of *Our Town*. Is it intermission at Weehawken Middle School, too? Is there a long line for the girls' room? I wonder how many women are waiting on line right this minute, for bathrooms in theatres all over the world.

A tousle-haired woman in a blue pantsuit takes out her cell phone and speed-dials. An awful thought strikes me, and I grab Cat's arm. "What if Miles is calling up Marion now, from a pay phone?"

"Um, Diana, I don't think there *are* any pay phones in the theatre."

"True. But you know what else? There might be more people backstage who know Marion Lavin."

"So?"

"*And* her niece Cindy." I look at Cat, letting the notion sink in. "Miles is completely sold, but what if it's just because he's, I don't know, nearsighted. Or he only met Cindy that one time, but there's somebody else who might —"

"Okay, okay. So what do we do? Skip going backstage?"

We look at each other, and both say at once, "*Naah.*"

The line for the ladies' room moves at a crawl. By the time we get back upstairs, the houselights are dimming. We rush down the aisle as fast as we can, which is faster for Cat than for me in my wobbly stilettos. My toes have begun to hurt and the backs of my legs feel all stretched. But as soon as the lights come back up on the stage, I've completely forgotten about my sore feet.

The romantic duet for Adam's character, Cody, and Angel reminds me of the balcony scene in *Romeo and Juliet*. Cody knows the sheriff is hard on his heels and his brothers have gone on ahead, but he won't leave town without saying good-bye to his angel. Taking his life in his hands, he climbs up a drainpipe and over porch roofs to appear at her window. Of course, in a musical, saying good-bye means a gorgeous duet.

As Adam and Sigrid Wilner, the luscious-voiced blonde who plays Angel, exchange passionate lines about the life they plan to share, I can't help imagining myself in Sigrid's place. That's *me* in that moon-dappled window, it's my hand he's clasping, it's my throat producing those heart-breaking sounds. I get utterly lost in the fantasy, seeing myself in her lacy white dressing gown, my hair piled high in those corkscrew curls. I can feel Adam's arms around my waist, the warm glow of the spotlights, the audience holding their breath as we sing. When our twinned voices soar up for the final high note, it's all I can do not to stand up and bow.

The applause brings me back to my senses, at least enough to see Cat and Miles on my left, clapping as hard as they can. I join in, clapping my hands. The show might stop dead in its tracks while the audience cheers and applauds, but the conductor's relentless, plunging us back into the story. The drums roll like gathering hoofbeats. The chase is on.

I'm at the edge of my seat as the set transforms yet again. Angel's room breaks apart as suddenly as their embrace, walls tumbling and flying as Cody races along the roof, swinging back down the drainpipe and onto his horse. In the dark we hear whinnying, hoofbeats, and music.

The stage lights flicker like lightning, revealing the stark silhouette of the rock where the other two brothers pace anxiously. Their singing is fraught: How long should we wait, is he already dead, we should never have left him.

At that instant, Cody arrives — and so does the posse, whirling onto the stage in a wild dance, all stomping boot heels and swirling chaps. My heart's in my throat, and I notice Cat clutching the arm of her chair.

The plot twists and gallops through several more turns. Cody is arrested and sentenced to death. At the gallows, a mysterious man in a black duster stages a last-minute rescue at knifepoint and is shot in the back by the sheriff. It turns out to be Angel, disguised as a man, her name now her destiny. Grief-stricken, Cody throws himself onto her knife. The two soul mates die in each other's arms as the music swells and the curtain comes down.

I don't think I've ever felt so many different emotions at once. I'm bawling my eyes out because it's so sad, but I'm also thrilled to the core. People are clapping and cheering all over the theatre. When the curtain opens again, I jump to my feet with the rest of the audience, pounding my hands till my palms are sore.

The actors come out of the wings in groups: first the dance hall girls and sheriff's posse, then people with more featured roles, then the two older brothers.

Finally it's Adam and Sigrid's turn. They enter from opposite wings and the crowd goes insane. As Adam steps to the front of the stage for his bow, with his hair tousled over his beautiful eyes, grinning as if he can't believe this is real, I hear Miles yell out a proud "Bravo!"

And then I remember: We're going *backstage*!

• • •

On the street, there's a cluster of autograph hunters and fans behind a wooden police barricade, but Miles walks right up to the stage door and speaks into an intercom. As soon as he gives the name "Kessler," the door opens wide. A gruff-looking doorman, chewing the butt of an unlit cigar, lets us inside. I can feel the crowd rustle and shift: Who are *they*? Who do *they* know?

The stage doorman is holding a clipboard with several names typed and scrawled on it. "You I got on my guest list," he rasps to Miles. "Who's these girls?"

"These young ladies are foreign-exchange students," Miles tells him. "They're my guests."

"Names?" He squints at me first.

"Cindy," I start, before panic grips me. I don't know Cindy's last name! Thinking fast, I break into a coughing fit, clutching at my throat as if something's gone down the wrong pipe.

"Are you okay?" Cat asks, and I'm proud to note that she's remembered her accent. I nod and keep coughing, the tears running down my cheeks as I sputter, "Cindy . . . Cin —"

"Don't try to speak," says Miles, bailing me out once more. "Cindy Harden. And this is Miss Catarina —"

"Catalina Portilla," says Cat quickly, using her mother's maiden name. As she spells it out — "*L-L-A*, like *tortilla*" — I catch my breath, wiping my eyes with the back of my hand. Too late, I remember I'm wearing mascara. I hope I haven't smeared it all over my face like a pirate raccoon.

But before I can worry too much about that, a trim woman wearing a headset appears and the doorman jerks his head toward the three of us. "Kessler."

She looks at us, nods, and says, "Follow me," leading us down a short hallway and into a large, darkened space. I gasp as I realize we're in the wings of a real Broadway theatre.

There are pieces of scenery standing around at odd angles, their canvas backs stenciled with names of scenes: *I-ii, Saloon; II-vi, Angel's Room*. There's a costume rack full of the clothes we just saw, and a wardrobe mistress is inspecting each piece under lights. Beside her, the prop master's setting six-shooters and saddlebags back on their labeled spots, getting ready for tomorrow's Act One.

144

The woman with the headset notices my excitement. "Want a look?" she asks, leading us onto the stage, where a stagehand is pushing a broom.

The space overhead is thrillingly high. Stray pieces of scenery hang down from the pipes used to fly them up and down, and there are clusters of spotlights hanging from catwalks. The most surprising of all is the back of the lush brocade curtain. From behind, it's a dull gray, and stenciled FIRE SAFETY. As we stand there, someone in the wings yells out, "Heads!" and the curtain goes up.

There I am, on a Broadway stage! I'm absolutely in heaven. Cat's gaping, too, and even Miles looks impressed. I stand staring out over the rows of plush seats, the two curving balconies, remembering the cheers and applause. Most of the seats are empty now, with custodians picking up discarded *Playbill*s and a few stragglers turning to look at the stage. In the orchestra pit, a man dismantles his tenor sax, setting it into its velvet-lined case.

I wonder, would anyone mind if I took a small bow? Just to see what it feels like. Before I can lose my nerve, I slide one foot back, bending the opposite knee as I lower my head. Next stop, Tony Award!

• • •

Whenever I thought about Broadway stars' dressing rooms, somehow I never imagined they'd be off a faded hallway up two flights of stairs. In old movies, the leading lady is always reclining on some giant chaise, waited on by a maid. There's a makeup mirror surrounded by flowers and photos, and plenty of seating for gentlemen callers. Sometimes there's even a piano.

Adam's dressing room is wedged between two or three others, each about the size of my bathroom. It's crowded with flowers and well-wishers, and feels totally chaotic. But the room doesn't matter at all. I can't take my eyes off his face.

Adam sits in a folding chair, flanked by two people who must be his parents, and three or four others, including the little redhead who asked for my autograph. Does everyone here know each other?

He's wearing a plain white T-shirt, damp at the neck where he's scrubbed off his stage makeup, and he looks relaxed, laughing and happy. The lit mirror picks up his profile, and both views are equally gorgeous. My breath seems to stop in my lungs and I actually wonder if I'm going to faint. That would be unbelievably lame and embarrassing.

Miles is the first through the door. Adam's parents beam at him as he booms, "You're a *star*!" Adam jumps out of his chair and embraces him warmly, thumping his back.

"You made it!"

"Of course I did. You were sensational!"

"Thanks, Pop." He looks over Miles's shoulder and notices me and Cat, skulking against the doorframe. "Who are your dates?" Adam asks with a mischievous grin.

Miles gestures at us to come in. "Cindy, Catalina? Meet Adam."

"That, that was so . . ." I manage to stammer. Where are my words? And when did my tongue get too big for my mouth? I hear Miles ask the rest of the family how they liked their box seats. I've got to say *something*, but my tongue won't move.

Cat pokes me in the ribs. "In *Ingles* you say, 'Awesome!'"

"So awesome," I echo. God, could I sound any more like an idiot? At least I remembered my accent.

"Thanks," Adam says. "I'm so glad you could come."
He really is a good actor, because he sounds just like he
means every word. I can't believe I'm standing two feet
away from him.

"Cindy is Marion Lavin's niece," Miles tells him.
"Maybe you've met her before?"

Adam shakes his head. "I would remember." He
holds out his hand, looking right at me with those gorgeous eyes.

My hand seems to rise by itself. In a second it's going
to touch his. . . .

If I really *do* faint, just bury me.

Chapter Eleven

I'm in an absolute haze as the after-show party relocates, in flocks of yellow cabs and a few town cars and limos, to Tavern on the Green, a restaurant surrounded by twinkle lights on the edge of Central Park.

Okay, sure, I've had crushes on actors before, but never on one that I've actually talked to. Or stammered at. Certainly not one who's shaken my hand.

If it weren't for my job at the cleaners, I think as our cab speeds away, none of this would have happened at all. I'd be on my way to the opening-night party for *Our Town* instead, with the girls changing costumes in the chorus room, while the boys all get dressed in the band room next door, between bass drums and sousaphones. Adam Kessler would just be a face in my locker. It's amazing the way things work out.

Ever since we wound up in the back of this cab — by some miracle, *not* with anyone from Adam's family or the rest of the cast, just the two of us — Cat has been talking nonstop. It's as if all the English that she hasn't spoken all night is pouring out of her mouth at once.

"All three of the brothers were cute, but those guys in the posse were *built*. Dancers' bodies, wow, they are *not kidding*. It's a good thing I didn't bring Jared. He would've put his hand over my eyes, that's no lie. Who was your favorite?"

The answer to this is so blatantly obvious that I can feel myself blushing. "The whole cast was great."

"Whole cast? *Someone's* putting that red in your cheeks, and it's not the whole cast. Let me guess. Did we go to his dressing room?"

Oh my god, am I really that easy to read? I must be, because Cat is grinning and pointing at me. "I knew it! And hey, the way he was looking at you? He is totally into you, too; I'm not making this up."

My heart pounds at her words. "That's ridiculous. He's the star of a Broadway show. I'm in eighth grade!"

"Not tonight," says Cat as our cab pulls up outside the restaurant. She looks at the time on her cell phone. "For the next . . . hour and ten minutes, we're both international glamour girls."

"Yes, but —"

"No buts," she says, paying the cabdriver. "And no English either. *No habla.*"

The restaurant is so elegant, I don't know what to do with myself. A hostess who looks like a supermodel takes our VIP invitation and checks off the name "Lavin (2)" on the guest list. "Welcome," she says with a smile.

Cat and I move uncertainly into the room. It's strange enough to be at a party where you don't know anybody, but it's even stranger to look across the room and *recognize* people you don't know. We keep whispering back and forth.

"Look, it's the saloonkeeper!"

"Wasn't she one of the dance hall girls?"

"Who's that guy with Tyra Banks? Is he famous?"

A live band is playing, even though nobody's out on the parquet dance floor yet. Everyone's too busy drinking and eating. There's a giant buffet table with mounds of food, and cater waiters in tuxes are passing out hors d'oeuvres on silver trays. "Salmon puff?" one of them says, and another asks, "Stuffed mushroom?"

We say yes to both. The salmon puff tastes a little like pigs-in-a-blanket with fish — kind of gross. But I love the stuffed mushroom, full of garlic and bread crumbs and melted cheese. Cat is grabbing an egg-rolly thing from a waiter's tray. I didn't think of it once while we were watching the show, but we never ate dinner. I'm suddenly starving.

"Let's check out the buffet," I say, and Cat nods with her mouth full. We get onto the line behind some rich businessman types who seem to be at the wrong party — all they can talk about is the stock market. I want to shout out, "Hello? Did you see the *show*?" but there isn't much point. Cat keeps craning her neck around the room, probably trying to locate those sheriff's posse dancers.

I'm looking for somebody, too. Adam was still signing autographs outside the theatre when our cab took off, but his family was already piling into a limo, so I'm sure they'll walk in any minute. Meanwhile, I load up my plate with everything I can fit: baked manicotti, chicken marsala, green beans almondine, mashed potatoes, spinach salad with bacon, and plenty of garlic bread.

We find a free table and sit down to eat. Suddenly there's a wave of cheers and applause in the room. Adam has entered — not with his proud family, but with his arm around Sigrid Wilner.

My stomach sinks. Of course. They're a *couple*. That's why he looked into her eyes that way, why their onstage duets were so passionate. He's in love with her offstage, too. And why wouldn't he be? She's beautiful, graceful, a Broadway professional. And she sings like . . . what else? Like an angel.

I'm sitting there with my mouth full of stuffed mani-cotti and I suddenly feel like I'm going to choke if I swallow it. But what else can I do? Spit it into a white linen napkin? What if somebody *saw* me? And what would I do with the napkin afterward, stuff it in one of the potted plants?

All around the room, people are standing to cheer. I want to join in, but my cheeks are stuffed as full as a hamster's with food I can't swallow. I turn my face down toward my plate, hoping no one will notice me. Somebody clinks on a crystal glass, and the rest of the room follows suit. A man toasts, "To the best cast on Broadway!"

Everyone whoops and applauds, and I look up. The cast clusters together for a photo. Flashbulbs are popping from every direction. I notice that Miles and the rest of the Kesslers are standing just inside the door, applauding with everyone else.

When the photo op's over, the cast splits apart. Adam goes right to his family, and Sigrid makes a beeline for some blond guy dressed in head-to-toe black. Could it be? I allow myself to hope as she crosses the room, past the band, which is playing an upbeat salsa tune. When she leaps into the blond guy's arms and kisses him, I'm suddenly able to swallow and eat food again. Call it a miracle.

Cat is not sitting back down. She jumped to her feet with the rest to applaud, and she's now staring right at the dance floor, where some of the posse guys and dance hall girls are strutting their stuff, with a few brave civilians joining the pros. A smile spreads across her face. She leans over my chair and says in a whisper, "I'll be right back, okay?"

Of course I say yes. And it is okay, for a while. I love watching Cat dance — she's almost as good as the professionals, and she's having the time of her life. Nelson would grin ear to ear if he saw how beautifully her dress moves on the dance floor.

I really am hungry, and the food on my plate is delicious. But I can't stop my eyes from drifting again and again toward Adam, who's never alone for an instant. It's not just his extended family: Wherever he turns, other actors come up to him, fans ask for autographs, businesspeople keep shaking his hand. It's clear that everyone in the room can tell he's a rising star, and wants to be near him. I keep daring myself to get up and talk to him, but I don't have the nerve. Maybe when Cat comes back to the table, we'll do it together.

But she doesn't come back, and I start to feel kind of awkward. I've finished my dinner and feel like I ate way too much, way too fast. My mouth tastes like garlic. Cat's taken up what looks like permanent residence on the dance floor, my feet hurt too much to join her, and even if I wasn't totally shy around strangers, there's nobody even remotely my age at this party. I take out my cell phone, about to text Jess at *her* opening-night party, but that seems a little pathetic. Besides which, she's probably having too much fun to pick up her phone. So I do what I always do: Check out people's outfits. This room is a gold mine.

A few minutes later, Miles spots me and waves. It looks like he's going to head for my table, but as soon as he takes a few steps, he's headed off by a woman in a red suit — I'd guess an agent or producer — who's been chatting up Adam. I'm hoping all three of them might come to sit at my table, but though Miles and Adam keep glancing over her shoulders, the woman in the power suit won't let them go. When she's joined by a very tanned man with a shaved head and glasses, I figure it's hopeless.

I wedge my toes back into Cat's torture stilettos, stand up, and cross the room, asking a waiter in my stupid accent, "Which way to the ladies', please?"

He sends me down a long hall. I push open the door, and am startled to see myself in the lounge's oversize mirror. I'd almost forgotten how stunning my gown is. In spite of the different fabric and color, Nelson has totally captured the elegant lines of The Dress. Seeing it with my upswept hair, pearls, and drop earrings is kind of a thrill. I lean forward to touch up my lipstick, and pop an Altoid into my mouth to take care of the garlic breath.

As soon as I'm done, though, I have the same feeling of *Now what?* As I step back into the hallway, I notice a door that leads out to the garden. Through the glass, I can see hedges cut into sculptures with twinkle lights twined through their branches. The cast-iron seats are all empty. It's too chilly tonight to sit under the stars, but a breath of fresh air seems like a perfect solution.

I wander out onto the patio. The sculpted evergreens give it a fantasy look, like something from Narnia, and the tiny white lights overhead, closely wound around every branch of the trees, add to the magic. I can see through the shrubs to the parking lot, where several limos are parked. A few of the drivers are sharing a cigarette, and I suddenly wish Mark was among them. *Well, he'll be here soon*, I think, looking up at the moon with a shiver.

I hear someone's footsteps behind me. I turn quickly, and almost fall off my stilettos. It's Adam.

"So what does it mean when the prettiest girl in the room is the only person who doesn't stand up when you enter the restaurant?"

Seventeen bells go off in my head. Did he just say "prettiest girl in the room"? More than that, did he actually notice, or care, if I stood up or not? The other fifteen bells must be from his grin, how his hair's falling over his forehead, his left eye, his right eye. . . .

"I had my mouth full," I say, and instantly wince at my blurt. Too much information. Especially since my mouth is *still* full of half-dissolved Altoid.

But Adam's grin just gets wider. "She's honest, too. And she's from — where, England?"

"London," I nod, feeling more and more helpless.

"My favorite city!"

Of course it is. And whatever I say next, you're going to see through.

I can see it all coming. It was one thing to improvise with kindly old Miles. It's another to stand here and look into Adam's amazing blue eyes — or are they a little bit green in the center? God, they look just like the ocean. What was I saying?

158

"Where does your family live?"

Okay, there it is. There's the noose, now go hang yourself. I've never been to London! I've never been to *New* England, much less the old one. Everything I know about London is from Harry Potter, or Mary Poppins, or —

"Wimpole Street," I tell Adam quickly. It's where my character went to live in *My Fair Lady*. Too late, I grit my teeth, hoping that Wimpole Street is still there, that regular people live on it, that Adam does not know the play inside out.

But he doesn't blink. He just shakes his head, smiling. "Wimpole," he says. "There's a name you don't hear every day."

That *smile*. I think it's erasing my brain. I can't think of a thing to say back.

"So, Cindy — it's Cindy, right?" Sort of. I nod and smile. "You're Marion's niece; that's so cool."

Okay. Stop nodding and smiling. You have to say *something* to him. "How do you know Marion?"

This seems safe enough, but he looks almost puzzled. "Everyone knows Marion. She's *the* agent to have, I mean, really the one."

She's an *agent*? My fake aunt is a real Broadway agent! Why didn't I Google her name when I had a chance? I should have done my research before I took her tickets.

I'm so busy beating myself up that it takes me a second to realize Adam's still talking. "I would never have gotten this job, or even a chance to audition, if Marion and Jeffrey weren't friends with my grandfather. I mean, the producers were after Zac Efron or someone from *American Idol*, not some high school kid from New Haven that nobody's heard of."

"They've heard of you now," I say. I can actually feel my eyes shining.

"I guess so." He shrugs. "It's all just so weird. You have all these daydreams about it, you know? Your big break? But you never expect it to actually happen. At least not to *you*."

Wow. He's even *humble*. Or knows how to sound like he is — with an actor, you're never quite sure. Adam might still be in high school, but it's not as if he's never been in a play — I've memorized every square inch of his bio, and I know he's done shows at Yale Rep and the Elm Shakespeare Festival, and guest-starred on *Gossip Girl* and a soap opera. It's not like somebody airlifted him straight from his high school production of *Bye Bye Birdie* to Broadway. Though I bet he was a great Conrad Birdie.

I'm nodding again. I can't seem to keep up my end of the dialogue here. I hope he can't see how I'm melting inside.

"So what brought you from Wimpole Street to New York?" he asks.

"Oh," I say. This is safe ground at least. "I'm on a foreign-exchange program."

"Really? Where are you going to school?"

Safe ground? No such thing. "Um . . . LaGuardia High School of Performing Arts." Good thing I've seen *Fame*.

Adam smiles warmly. "So you're a performer? What kind?"

"I'm an actress."

"That's great!" He sounds truly excited. Why does he have to be humble, and friendly, and *nice*? It was hard enough keeping my head straight when he was just gorgeous. "What's your favorite role?"

This is a trick question. I can't say *My Fair Lady* — dead giveaway on the accent front — and I'm not about to bring up *Cafeteria Daze*. Well, he didn't say favorite role that you've actually *played*, so I tell him my real favorite.

"Emily Webb in *Our Town*."

His beautiful eyes open wide. "Mine was George Gibbs."

We stare at each other. If this was a movie, this would be where the two leading actors would kiss. I've never kissed a boy, much less a star whose picture I've got in my locker. I suddenly wonder if Kayleigh kissed Ethan tonight, and then wonder how any part of my mind could have gone there when I'm having this incredible moment with Adam Kessler. When he's looking at me with those ocean blue eyes and assuming I'm someone I'm not. When I'm thirteen years old in my friend's borrowed shoes that are killing my feet, and a dress made of leftovers.

Why does real life always have to kick in?

The ready-to-kiss close-up passes, but not the way we gaze at each other, standing there under the twinkle lights. I suddenly realize I can still hear the party inside. The band's playing something romantic.

"Do you . . . Would you like to dance?" Adam asks.

"Here?"

He shrugs his shoulders. "Why not?"

Let's see. Because I can barely walk in these shoes, let alone really move? Because I just watched you dancing onstage for two hours and you're so far out of my league it's insane? And, oh yes, did I mention that I'm in eighth grade? Or that I'm having feelings I really don't know how to handle, at all, at all?

"I'd love to," I say.

Adam holds out his hand and I take it. That what-if-I-faint? thing is starting to kick in again as he steps closer and gently rests his other hand on one side of my waist. He looks into my eyes, hesitating a moment.

"Would you like to take off those shoes?" he asks tentatively. "If it won't make your feet too cold?"

Am I blushing bright red? It sure feels like I am. "I don't want to step on the hem of my dress," I say, telling the truth, at least part of it. I also don't want to suddenly look like his kid sister. Adam nods.

"I couldn't dance two steps in those heels. I'm impressed."

"Don't be impressed until I don't step on you," I say.

"I'll take it slow." And he does. There almost isn't a point where we seem to start dancing together. One minute we're not, the next minute we are. I don't know how it happened, but it feels like heaven on earth. It was dreamy enough sitting in a dark audience, watching him dance and pretending that I was his Angel, but here we are, under the nearly full moon, with all those white lights swirling over our heads like stars.

Two headlights sweep over the patio, bathing us in double spotlights till the car pulls up at the restaurant's front door. It's an airport car service. From the back door slides an elegant leg, draped in a chocolate-bronze fabric that I'm shocked to recognize. When a tall, dark-haired woman gets out of the cab and pauses to throw a dramatic shawl over her shoulders, there's no way to mistake it: She's wearing The Dress!

I must have gone stiff, because Adam twists to look over his shoulder. "It's Marion!" he exclaims. "She must have gotten a later flight."

Help!!!

Chapter Twelve

This is the thing about lying. One lie leads to the next, and the next, and before you know it, you're in so far over your head that one speck of truth can bury you. Here's a short list of what goes through my head, all at once, when I find out Marion Lavin is here:

— How long until midnight?

— Why isn't Mark here yet?

— How can I go back to get Cat off the dance floor without Adam, or Miles, pushing me toward my "aunt"?

— If she sees me, we're *dead*.

And:

— Does this mean I have to stop dancing with Adam?

"Let's go say hello," he says, taking my arm.

I hesitate. Over his shoulder, I see the lit clock on the top of a skyscraper. Twelve minutes till midnight. I could buy some time by asking to finish this dance first (plus I'd get to finish this dance!), but Marion's probably already inside the restaurant. She might even be talking to Miles, though, hopefully, he's still across the room from the door. Probably best to move quickly, grab Cat and get out.

Except Mark isn't here yet. What if Adam and Marion follow us to the parking lot?

I don't know what to do, so I just chirp, "Okay." Adam ushers me back to the door, where he pauses and looks at me.

"Promise we'll come back out here for an encore."

Oh, help, do I have to lie *again*? I choose my words carefully. I look into Adam's amazing blue eyes and tell him, with all my heart, "I would love that."

He smiles, holding the door open. My heart's pounding under my ribs as we head up the hall, toward the door to the bathrooms and kitchen. A willowy African-American dancer I recognize from the cast is about to go into the ladies' room. She smiles at Adam. "*There* you are! Everyone's looking for you."

Is "everyone" Miles and Marion? I swallow hard, and tell Adam, "Excuse me a moment. I have to . . ." I make a vague wave toward the bathroom door, and he gets it.

"I'll wait right here."

"No, don't. They're all waiting for you. I'll see you inside in a minute." Possibly as I'm being dragged out by bouncers.

Adam looks disappointed. "Yeah, okay. But if I get swarmed again . . ."

"I'll come and get you." Now that *is* a lie, but it works. He heads back toward the restaurant, and I dash into the ladies' room. The tall dancer's about to go into a stall. I shout out, "Excuse me!"

She turns, surprised. "Me?"

"Would you do me a huge favor?"

She's looking at me with a frown. "Weren't you British a minute ago?"

Busted! I knew I'd slip sooner or later. No time to explain. "My friend, with the orange satin dress, black hair, she's been dancing with you guys all night?"

"Sure. She's a great dancer."

"Could you please go get her? Tell her to bring her purse. Tell her it's urgent."

The dancer's face softens with understanding. "Oh, I get it. It's a girl thing, right?"

"It's not that. It's urgent. It's totally, utterly, save-my-life urgent."

She looks me up and down. "Okay. I'll get your friend for you soon as I'm done." And she goes into the stall.

It seems like a year and a half till she comes out and washes her hands.

"I'm on the case. What's your friend's name?"

"Catalina. Thank you *so* much!" As she's leaving, an afterthought strikes me. "Oh, she understands English."

"Yeah, okay," she says, looking at me like I'm nuts as she goes out the door.

I pull out my cell phone and stare at the time. It's 11:52. While I'm waiting for Cat to show up, I try to focus on an escape plan that might actually work, instead of the worst-case scenarios that keep flooding my brain. What if Marion comes to the bathroom and finds her fake niece in front of this mirror, wearing a knockoff of her dress? And I stole her tickets, too. What if she calls the police?

After what's only three minutes but seems an eternity, Cat bursts in through the door. "What's the problem?"

"Marion Lavin just got here."

Her eyes get enormous. "Fur Coat Lady?"

I nod. "And she's wearing The Dress." I point to the halter neckline and lace trim on mine.

"You're kidding me!"

"I wish. The garden out back looks onto the parking lot. I think we can get to it through the shrubs. Go out and see if Mark's limo is there yet."

"Why don't you come with me?"

"Because Adam might look for me there."

"Adam, as in *Adam Kessler*? Is that where you've —"

"Later. Go. Hurry."

Cat goes and comes back in a heartbeat. "Not yet. But you know what else? I left my shawl at our table."

"You're kidding me."

"Tasha said to bring my purse. How was I supposed to know?"

"We *can't* go back into the restaurant!"

"My *abuela* sent me that shawl from Guatemala. I am not gonna leave it. No way." Cat folds her arms. I can tell she's not kidding.

"All right, here's what we do," I say, thinking out loud. "Go get your shawl. If you see Adam or Miles talking to a woman in a floor-length brown silk, we bust out through the shrubs whether Mark's limo is there or not. If we have to, we'll take a cab. Go!"

Cat nods and leaves, while I hyperventilate. What if they see her? It's hard to miss someone in flaming orange satin. What if Marion follows her back down the hall? What if, what if, what if. I position myself just inside the door, checking my phone again. Two minutes left.

Cat bursts back in, wild-eyed. "Shrubs!" We rush out to the garden and make a beeline for the shrubs. How did neither one of us notice that green wooden fence right behind them? We can't get through.

"What do we do?" Cat practically screams.

"Hallway." I grab her and run.

"But they're coming!" Sure enough, as soon as we enter the hall, we see Marion, Adam, and Miles coming right toward us. We're trapped!

Just then, a waiter swings out though the kitchen door, holding a large tray at shoulder height. His approach slows them down and I see an escape route. "Come on!" I hiss, yanking Cat through the swinging door into the kitchen.

It's a hive of activity, with cooks in whites juggling sizzling saucepans and speed-dicing carrots. The whole prep line swivels and stares as we charge down the center aisle. "Sorry, just passing through!" I yell, teetering on my stiletto heels. One of the dishwashers almost drops a full rack of clean china.

"You can't be in here!" fumes a high-hatted chef, but we've already passed him and run through the screen door to the loading dock. From here, we can see the front entrance and parking lot — where, bless his heart, Mark is pulling his stretch limo into the queue. The clock on the building above clicks to midnight.

"Run!" yells Cat. "We're supposed to be waiting for him. He'll take off without us!" She pelts down the ramp toward the parking lot. I follow, but can't negotiate the steep ramp in my heels. I kick them off, scoop them up in my arms, and run barefooted down the ice-cold cement, hoping like crazy I'm not going to trip on my hem.

Mark's spotted Cat, who's running right at the limo and waving her arms. He gets out to open the door for her. I can't hear what she says, but he nods and gets back at the wheel, leaving the door open. Cat dives inside. As I run pell-mell over the parking lot, I see Adam charge out the front door of the restaurant.

"Wait!" he shouts. "Cindy!"

Of course I trip, and both shoes go flying. As I stumble back to my feet, I can see Adam heading right toward me, and Miles and Marion framed in the doorway. I grab the one shoe within reach, yell, "I'm so sorry!" and hurtle full-speed at the limo. As soon as I'm through the door, Mark peels out fast.

"Oh my god!" Cat keeps saying. "Ohmygod ohmygod!" The last thing I see, as I twist to look out through the window, is Adam. He's still running after the limo, but slows to a stop, realizing that he can't catch up. His arms sag to his sides, and he looks so sad that my heart leaps up into my throat. I watch him through the glass as he bends down to pick up my shoe.

"That was *sick*!" Cat beams as the limo zooms back through the tunnel. "I never had so much fun in my life."

"You're not mad about losing your shoe?"

"Well, I didn't say *that*."

"You saw where it landed. If I went back for it, we wouldn't be in this limo."

"Yeah, yeah," says Cat. "The main thing is we got away with it."

I wish she was right, but I still have a lot more to get away with. For starters, I'm a bedraggled mess. I scraped both my knees when I tripped and fell, and the hem of my dress is not only muddy but actually torn, where I slammed it inside the door of the limo. Nelson is going to be furious.

Apparently he's not alone. The first thing Jess says when I call on my cell phone is, "Fay's on the warpath."

"When did she call?"

"Ten minutes ago. When they got home and found someone else babysitting."

Oh, great. Now Elise will be mad at me, too. "Can I still come to your house and change my clothes? The last thing I need is for Fay to see me in this dress."

"Sure," says Jess, clipped. "I was good in *Our Town*. Thanks for asking."

Add Jess to the list. Is there anyone who *isn't* mad at me?

I give Mark directions to Jess's house. "No can do," he says. "I'm on a tight round-trip. I've got time for one stop and that's *it*."

"I'll give you a ride in the van," says Cat. "If it starts."

Somebody up there must love us, because Jared's van *does* start. The engine's as loud as a motorcycle, but it gets us to Jess's. As soon as we pull up, she runs outside, wild-eyed.

"Fay's on her way over!"

"What?" I grab the bag with my clothes, yell a quick, "Thanks!" to Cat and charge after Jess, who's talking a mile a minute. She's wearing her nighttime retainer, so her words come out lispy and garbled.

"I called twice on your cell, but you didn't —"

"The muffler is broken, I couldn't hear." We're inside, in the kitchen. Jess dumps my clothes out on the table.

"She'll be here any minute. Quick." She unzips my dress, pulling it over my head. "This is *gorgeous*, wow!"

"Hide it." I step into my jeans, quickly zipping them up as Jess rolls up the dress and stashes it inside the shopping bag. I pull my sweater over my head in the nick of time, just as her brother, Dash, comes down the stairs in pajamas.

"Could you *knock?*" yells Jess.

"Who wants to see you two changing?" he says, covering his eyes with one hand when he spots me straightening my sweater. "*So* gross!"

"Get out of here, creep," Jess says, swatting at him.

"Thought you might need this." He throws an *Our Town* program onto the table and heads back upstairs as I reach up and pull out my hair clips.

"Makeup," says Jess, making a dash for the sink and pulling about four feet of paper towels off the rack. As she tears one off and wets it, I perch on a kitchen chair, frantically pulling on my socks and sneakers.

"So the show was good?"

"Most of it stunk," she says, blotting my eye makeup off as I struggle to tie up my sneakers by feel. "*I* was good. The worst part was the audience. Practically no one showed up. Oh, no! It's *her*!"

I see the SUV's high headlights pull into the driveway. "How's my face?"

"Wet." Jess pushes a dry towel into my hands and kicks the shopping bag with my gown out of sight under the counter. "I'll bring this to school." I nod, blotting my face, probably smearing the rest of my makeup all over it, as I hear a car door slam. I pick up the *Our Town* program, clutching it to my chest for protection.

Fay doesn't even knock. Her face is a frightening color of red. "You come with me this instant," she growls, grabbing the program out of my hand. I can feel her eyes rest on my neck, and too late, I realize that I'm still wearing Mom's pearls.

Chapter Thirteen

The next two days are the worst weekend I've ever had. Fay's furious at me for leaving her precious twins with a stranger (even though they had the time of their lives). But the real black hole is my dad. If he uses the phrase "disappointed in you" one more time, I'm going to curl up on the carpet and stop taking breaths. Even when he's not giving me lectures about trust and responsibility and telling the truth, the look in his eyes makes me want to weep. I can deal with Fay being angry at me — she usually is — but Dad's sadness is too much to bear.

I'm grounded, of course, with a long list of chores. I'm forbidden to pick up the phone, which means Jess and the rest of my friends think I'm being disgustingly rude and ignoring them. Fay's taken away my cell and my laptop, just to be sure I won't sneak any messages. There's another performance of *Our Town* tonight, and two more next weekend, but you can bet I won't be going — not only because Dad and Fay think I saw it last night, but because I won't be allowed out of the house for anything but school and work, for — they won't even tell me exactly how long. I could be grounded till I turn eighteen.

Fay's got me scrubbing the bathroom floors. I don't actually mind this; it's something to do. The physical work makes me tired, which is better than moping. But as I kneel on the tiles, working a bristle brush over the stains, it's impossible to keep my thoughts from drifting back to Friday night, to that elegant whirl of satin and limos and flashbulbs, and that magical time in the restaurant garden when Adam took me in his arms to dance under the stars. How can this lump of detergent-streaked misery, down on her knees in a T-shirt and sweatpants, possibly be the same girl who did *that*?

It gets even worse Sunday morning. Dad drives to LaToria's Bakery, just like he does every week, to bring home fresh pastries for breakfast — cinnamon sweet rolls or cherry-cheese Danish or coffee cake studded with pecans and icing — and the Sunday papers. Dad always picks up the local paper for full-color funnies, movie listings, and New Jersey news, and the *New York Times* for everything else.

In the old days, when my grandparents still lived nearby, Papa and Nonni would come by after church and we'd eat a big breakfast together and sit around reading different sections of both papers. Mom did the crossword puzzle first thing, with a special red pen. Dad went for the Week in Review and the Sports section. Papa and I read the funnies, and then he moved on to Automobiles ("that new Lexus has very sharp lines") while I read all our horoscopes. Nonni would buzz around, wrapping leftovers and doing the dishes, though everyone begged her to stop. As soon as Mom finished the crossword, the two of us sat side by side at the dining room table with our holy of holies, the *Times* Arts & Leisure, looking at ads for the new Broadway shows.

Of course this tradition wavered when Mom got sick, and it fell by the wayside completely when Papa and Nonni moved to Florida. But Dad still insists on buying both papers, and I still pore over the Arts & Leisure. So this Sunday, after I've done all the dishes and cleaned up the kitchen, I go into the living room and ask Dad for my favorite section.

There it is, right on the front page: a photo of Adam in costume, gazing into the eyes of his Angel, with his hand on the side of her waist, just the way he held me. Right inside is a full-page ad, with more photos and quotes from the rave reviews.

It's a smash hit! "An instant classic," reads one banner headline, and another, "A star is born!"

And I was there, at the opening night. I danced with that star. Whatever else happens, I'll still get to cherish those memories.

That thought doesn't help me get through school, though, where Jess thrusts the shopping bag with my dress into my locker without a word, as if it were my fault I wasn't allowed to call or IM her all weekend, or go to the second show Saturday night.

And it certainly doesn't help me get through my first afternoon back at work.

Elise is hanging her pink hoodie inside her locker when I come in through the back door. "My stepsisters said you were the best sitter ever," I tell her gratefully. "I really can't thank you enough."

"No, you really can't," she replies coolly. "Why didn't you tell me your parents were going to get home before you did?"

"I didn't know." It's the truth, but I still feel guilty.

Elise fixes me with a withering look. "Didn't care is more like it. Your father's my *boss*, and you got me in trouble with him."

"I'm so sorry, Elise. I really —"

"Whatever. You had your adventure. Just please leave me out of the next one, okay? I haven't been fired yet, and I'm not taking any more chances." She turns and walks out of the room.

I stand still for a moment. It's hard to imagine how I could feel any worse, but then I look down at the bag in my hands. I still have to tell Nelson I ruined his beautiful gown. Well, I can't bring it to Tailoring without MacInerny seeing me and asking questions, so it's probably safest to leave it right here in my locker till I get a chance to speak to him in private.

An hour or so later, he comes through the workroom

on his way to the men's room. I leave my laundry cart right in the aisle and rush after him, trying to catch up before he goes through the door.

"Nelson?"

He arches an eyebrow. "Oh, you're still speaking to me? That's strange, because I didn't hear from you all weekend long, not even a thanks-for-the-limo. Cat called me *twice*."

"My stepmother grounded me. No phone or Facebook."

"And?"

"And thanks for the limo. The gown. Thanks for everything."

"That's a little more like it," he says.

I wish I could leave it right there, but I have to be honest. "The hem's kind of torn," I say, wincing. "I tripped. And it caught in the door. I'm so sorry."

"Where is it now?"

"Meet me next to the soda machine," I say, and go into the locker room. I take out the shopping bag and wait in the hallway for Nelson.

He frowns when he sees me standing there with the bag, but says nothing. He just reaches inside and gingerly pulls out the mud-streaked, torn, wrinkled mass that was my Nelson Couture gown, holding it up at full length. It's really a mess.

"I'm so, so sorry," I tell him again.

"Promise me something, Diana," says Nelson. "Whatever you do in this lifetime, promise you'll *never* put something I've sewn in a shopping bag that says KMART."

For the rest of the day, I'm a model employee. I'm there before anyone needs me; I do my work so quickly and silently that MacInerny is almost suspicious. I don't talk to anyone, not even Cat.

She catches up with me at the end of the day, though, when we're both hanging up our smocks. Elise has cold-shouldered me all afternoon, and when she punches her time card and leaves without even saying good-bye, I feel awful.

Cat shrugs. "She'll get over herself."

"I don't think so."

She tugs on her denim jacket. "Diana, you gotta get out of this funk, okay?"

"Everyone's mad at me."

"*I'm* not. Even though you left one of my Baby Phats on the wrong side of the river. Hey, you think Adam's still got it? We could do like a road trip, go meet him outside the stage door. Go up to his dressing room." She drops a suggestive wink, bumping my arm. I am not in the mood.

"I'm not taking road trips to anywhere, ever again."

"Don't give up so easy. He *liked* you, for real. And you promised you'd give him an encore."

"The girl he wanted to dance with was Cindy, not me," I tell her. "I've got to go home with my dad."

I'm a model employee at home as well. I serve and clear dinner without being asked, and speak only when spoken to. I don't rise to the bait when Ashley declares, for the ninety-fifth time, that my clothes stink of chemicals. I even help Brynna with math homework.

As we sit side by side in the living room, doing equations, Dad turns on the news and sits down with a sigh. I tune out the newscaster's voice as he drones on about the economy. And then suddenly I hear a voice I'd know anywhere.

On the TV screen, Adam is crooning a love song from *Angel*. As costumed dancers whirl, kick, and spin, an announcer intones, "There's a new generation on Broadway, and everyone's falling in love."

The ad cuts to a shot of the marquee, with sound bites from thrilled theatergoers. Right behind one of them, someone in white-and-black satin is signing a red-haired girl's program. It's *me*!

I manage to stop myself from screaming out loud, but I'm not the only person who's noticed.

"That young woman looks a little like you," says my dad.

"Hardly," says Fay in dismissive tones. "She must be someone important."

I don't care what anyone thinks. I jump up from the table and pound upstairs, slamming the door to my bedroom. I pull open the drawer where I've hidden Mom's necklace and the *Playbill* from *Angel*, and throw myself onto my bed, sobbing. I've never felt so alone in my life.

Chapter Fourteen

It takes all day Tuesday for Jess to thaw out and start speaking to me again. Meanwhile, I overhear *Our Town* gossip from every direction. Sara tells me the first weekend's shows were less than half full on both nights. The drama club has to sell more seats this weekend or Ms. Wyant says we can't have a spring play. That would be awful. Unthinkable.

The word on the show is mixed. Everybody says Riley Jackson, who's playing the Stage Manager, did an incredible job. The slacker milkman forgot half his lines, and one of the mourners' umbrellas got stuck. But the main gossip item — Did George and Emily kiss at their wedding? — is answered as soon as I see Kayleigh Carell parade into English class, holding hands not with Zane, but with Ethan.

Evidently they did kiss on opening night. Zane made good on his threat to break up with Kayleigh, and the obvious happened: The stage romance turned into a real one. I remember the way Adam gazed into Sigrid's eyes onstage, making their love so convincing that when I saw them walk into the opening gala together, I assumed they must be a real couple.

I wonder how actors — or anyone else, for that matter — can tell when it's real. If you feel the way I did when Adam was dancing with me in the garden, like there's not enough oxygen in the world to fill up your lungs, like you're suddenly running a fever, are you really in love?

Because I've never felt that with anyone else, not even the crushes I've had. And because, even now, with the red carpet pulled out from under my feet and a serious crash landing back to reality, I feel the same way every time I remember his face.

There's a line in *Our Town* I adore. It's from the scene in the soda fountain, right after Emily tells George off for acting stuck-up. Instead of getting mad, he tells her she's right, and that he's going to change, and little by little, without either of them ever using the word, they discover how much they're in love with each other. At one point, George blurts out, "I always thought of you as one of the chief people I thought about." I love how awkward that is, because it's exactly how awkward you feel when someone becomes . . . well, *the* chief person you think about. All day long.

Things have settled a little at work, too, though Elise is still keeping her distance. When she's at the customer counter, my pickup runs are all business, and even when she's in the back bagging clothes, which is always a little more private, we don't really talk to each other.

Today it's Cat's turn to work at the bagging machine, at least until after our break, which we decide to take up on the roof even though there's a chill in the air. The steam that comes up from the ventilation fans keeps us both warm, and we get to look out at my favorite view. It's even more special to me now, since midtown Manhattan is full of great memories. Cat takes out her customer order pad and tears off a pink sheet. She writes something on it, then folds it up into a paper airplane and flies it right off the roof.

"Make a wish," she says, holding the pad out toward me, but I don't see the point. I shake my head and tell her thanks anyway.

"Oh, come on. What's the harm?" She pushes the pad toward me again.

"Fine," I say irritably. I write something so tiny that no one could read it, fold the paper into the familiar angles, and toss it out into the wind, where it takes an immediate nosedive. It figures. Even my wishes are grounded.

"We better get back to work," I say. "Mac'll go postal if we're both late." Cat nods and we climb down the iron rungs.

My dad's out in Brooklyn today, meeting a supplier of green-cleaning products, which means MacInerny's in charge. She's been strutting around the front office all day like a bantam rooster, driving everyone nuts, but before she sends Elise to the back and starts Cat at the customer counter, she does something I've never seen her do before.

She takes the cash drawer out of the register that Elise has been using.

"I want to count this," she says, in a tone that implies that she's certain to find something wrong when she does.

This is more than I can stand. I've barely spoken aloud on the job for two days, especially today with MacInerny in charge, but my voice rings out loud and clear. "Elise is the most honest person I know."

Miss MacInerny fixes me with a furious glare, but it doesn't faze me in the least. She's a pussycat next to my stepmother.

"Nobody asked your opinion," she snaps.

"It's not an opinion. It's true. Elise hasn't done anything wrong and she never would. You have no right to be so suspicious."

The sewing machines have stopped working as Nelson, Loretta, and Sadie all turn on their stools. Cat is staring at me with her jaw dropped, and Elise's face is an uneasy mix of gratitude and embarrassment.

"I'm doing my job. I suggest you do yours," MacInerny snaps.

"Then lay off Elise."

Elise starts to say something, but MacInerny steamrolls right over her, still focused on me. "You do not take that tone with me. I am your supervisor, and when your father is out of his office, I am the boss."

"My father would never accuse an employee of stealing unless he had —" I break off mid-sentence and stare with my eyes bulging. The customer doorbell just sounded, and there on the threshold, with an *Angel* program in one hand and a shoe in the other, is *Adam Kessler*!

I let out a squawk that's pure Jersey girl. He probably just overheard my real voice!

What is he *doing* here?? I can't let him see me in this hideous pastel green smock, with no makeup, my hair pulled back in a sloppy ponytail!

Maybe he hasn't noticed me yet, or thinks I'm Cindy's kid sister. Turning my face to the wall, I scuttle as fast as I can toward the swinging doors into the workroom, past a head-swiveling Cat.

"Hey, that's my Baby Phat!" Cat exclaims.

"Excuse me," says Adam, shoving the shoe into her hands and vaulting over the counter as MacInerny

191

shrieks, "Young man! You can't do that! Young man! Employees only!"

But Adam has already followed me into the crowded workroom. People stop working and stare, leaving dryer doors open and irons on shirts, as I dodge around carts full of laundry and duck under plastic-bagged clothes swishing by overhead.

Adam's hot on my heels. Mr. Chen shouts, "Careful! Hot!" as we zoom past his steam presser. All I want to do is get into the bathroom, where I can hide.

"Sorry!" Adam yells as he zigzags around the stupefied group at the sorting table. He's gaining on me. Just up ahead, Chris is blocking the aisle with a rolling mop bucket, cleaning up a spilled Pepsi. I skid to a stop.

"Don't make me follow you into the ladies' room," Adam says, catching hold of my arm. "I lost you once in a restaurant kitchen. I'm not going to lose you again."

"How did you *find* me?" I gasp.

He grins and holds up the autographed program. "My cousin Ruby's. You signed your real name."

I can feel myself starting to sway on my feet. It could be the heat from industrial dryers, or it could be . . . *him*.

Adam catches me, lifting me into his arms and carrying me back through the crowded workroom. I can't help it. My arms go around his neck.

Nelson lets out a whistle and claps. He's standing just inside the doors with Cat and the rest of the tailors. They're all watching as if we're a movie.

Loretta sighs, "So romantic!" and Sadie's hand covers her heart. Cat is beaming. If she had a thought bubble over her head, it would read, "What did I tell you?"

I lower my voice so no one but Adam can hear me above the machine noise. "My name isn't Cindy," I tell him, but he doesn't blink.

"I know."

"I'm not Marion's niece."

"I know." God, is he gorgeous. Can I just keep looking at him?

"I'm not really from London."

He's grinning from ear to ear. "Duh!"

I look into his eyes, wishing I could just leave it at that. But there's one more thing I have to set straight, even though it'll change everything.

"Adam?" I breathe.

"Yes?" He's smiling right at me.

"I'm thirteen years old."

Adam stops. Puts me down. He takes a step backward and looks at me as if he's seeing me for the first time. Not Cindy in satin and pearls and borrowed high heels, but me, as I actually am. Messy ponytail, blue jeans, and sneakers with two different laces. A girl with a crush on an actor.

"You're only *thirteen*?"

I nod guiltily. "I'm in eighth grade."

Adam lets out a long deep breath, looks me right in the eye, and says, "You're a pretty good actress."

Sad as I am, those words bring some joy to my heart.

"It was my agent who put it together," says Adam.

I wince. "Marion Lavin?"

He nods with a wicked smile. "Your quote unquote aunt." He reaches to take a french fry off my plate, and my heart skips a little, even though he's not flirting at all anymore. He's still friendly and open, but suddenly Adam seems much older and I feel much younger.

We're sharing a booth at Sam's Diner. I already took my break with Cat, but MacInerny must not have realized that, since she just sent me out on another. Or maybe she just wants me out of her sight.

Whatever. I've got ten minutes with Adam, and that's enough.

He's still talking. "Marion knew you weren't her niece Cindy, of course, but none of us could figure out how this Diana Donato who signed Ruby's program got hold of Marion's tickets. And then she remembered your father's last name. And the coat she'd dropped off when she picked up her dress from the cleaners."

"I did try to call her," I say. "But her housekeeper said she was out of the country, and I thought her tickets would just go to waste."

"I'm so glad they didn't," says Adam.

"Me, too." I can't look into those eyes without getting dizzy. I can actually feel myself blushing. I hope my cheeks aren't bright red.

Adam picks up the check from the table. "I've got to get back to the city in time for my show. But you know, if you'd like to see *Angel* again —"

"If? Are you kidding??"

He grins at me. "Really?"

"I *loved* it. I mean, I just totally, totally loved it." Wow. Inarticulate much?

"Well, if you'd like to come back with a friend or your parents, leave a message for me at the stage door. I could get you some house seats."

"OMG! That would be *awesome*!" If I hadn't already told him I was thirteen, he'd have no trouble guessing it now. But I'm totally blown away. Go back and see *Angel* in house seats? Get to see Adam again? This is better than I could imagine. If I could just wave a magic wand and make myself be seventeen, life would be perfect.

But there aren't magic wands, not real ones at least, and I'm not Adam's age. No matter how much I might dream about dating him, it will never be more than a dream. He takes out his wallet and puts down some money — a really big tip, but why not? He's a Broadway star.

Maybe someday I'll be one myself, but right now, I'm a stagestruck eighth grader who works at the cleaners next door. And the magical part is that somehow that's almost enough.

Chapter Fifteen

All through the next workday, I'm walking on eggshells, but nobody mentions a word to my dad, not even Miss MacInerny. I guess she can't be bothered with celebrities leaping over the customer counter when there's a complaint about *me* she can air. Nelson overheard her telling my dad I was "disrespectful" and "fresh-mouthed," which sounds like I'm using mint breath spray, but hey. As long as she keeps her mouth shut about Adam, I'm fine with whatever she says about me.

So when Dad asks me to step into his office and closes the door, I quake in my sneakers. Maybe she said something else, out of earshot of Nelson. I'm already in nine kinds of trouble for sneaking away to the opening night of *Our Town*. If he found out that I really went to New York

197

City with Cat, I can't even imagine what Fay's going to do to me. I could be under arrest.

I sneak a peek at Dad's face as he sits back down in his desk chair. He doesn't look furious, but his expression is stern.

"I've heard some things I don't care for, Diana." I hold my breath. Here it comes. My life is *over*. "Did you use rude language to Miss MacInerny?"

I look at him, speechless. Is that *all*? I'm so relieved I want to break into song, but I try to stay in character. After all, Adam Kessler said I could act.

"I'm sorry," I tell my dad. "She was accusing Elise of stealing."

"Did she actually use those words?"

I try to remember. "Well, no. She just said she was going to count out the cash in Elise's drawer."

"Which is part of her job."

Really? "I didn't know that."

"One of us does it after every shift at the register. It's standard business procedure." I feel like an idiot. Dad leans across his desk. "Even if you felt your supervisor was in the wrong, it isn't your place to confront her. Especially not in front of the rest of the staff."

"I won't do it again," I say, feeling contrite.

Dad's look softens. "I know Joy can seem harsh at times, especially with you girls, but she is the rock this place rests on. Your grandpapa depended on her, and so do I. I don't want to burden you with things you don't need to know, but she's had a lot of tragedy in her life. The world isn't carved into good guys and bad guys, like it is in the movies. Or one of your plays."

I nod, wondering what kind of tragedy made MacInerny turn Joyless. Well, some other time. There's something else I want to ask Dad, but this may not be the right moment. He keeps looking at me, though, as if he expects me to say something else.

"Go ahead," he says. "I'm listening." He really knows me inside out.

"Well, it's this," I say, pausing. I know what I'm going to ask is outrageous. I'm already grounded for going to see it (supposedly), but I can't stand the idea of missing *Our Town*, especially when everybody's been trying so hard to sell tickets. "Is there any way in the world you'd consider ungrounding me, just for one night, so I could go to the Saturday show of the play?"

He raises his eyebrows. I barrel on anyway, gathering speed. "Jess and Ethan and Riley are all in it, and it's closing night. I know it's ridiculous even to ask, I know what I did wasn't right and that lying about it made it even worse, but I really —"

"Okay," says Dad.

"I'll do anything you and Fay ask me —" I grind to a halt, staring at him. "Did you say okay?"

"I did," says my father. "But on one condition."

I nod eagerly. "Anything."

"Be nicer to Fay." I'm sure my face falls, but he keeps on going. "I know how much you wanted to be in the play, and that it was hard for you to give it up. But you did it, for me and our family. Fay's part of our family now."

I look at him sharply. How can he say that? She'll never be part of my family, never. Dad sighs. "I know that's not easy for you to accept, and she can be very hard on you sometimes. I see that. But I also see how hard you push her away, and I'm not sure you know how that hurts her. Just try to be nicer."

I look at my feet. I'm really not sure I can do this. Dad reaches across his desk, taking my hand. "Diana, I know how much you miss your mother. I miss her, too. Every day. But we can't have her back."

"I know, Dad," I whisper. I'm thinking again of Act Three in *Our Town*, when Emily gets to come back for one day and watch her old life. I can feel my eyes stinging. It's probably just as well I'm not playing that part — if I started crying onstage I might never be able to stop. There are some things you can't fix. I look back up at my dad and nod. "I'll do my best."

"Thank you," he says, and he squeezes my hand and lets go. I stand up and walk out of Dad's office, passing a sign for a fund-raising raffle sponsored by Fay's Junior League. And I'm suddenly hit with the perfect idea. There *is* something I might be able to fix, after all.

It takes just one phone call to set up the house seats. The tickets arrive in an overnight mailer, along with a program signed by the whole *Angel* cast, and two autographed 8 x 10 photos of Adam. One's for the poster I'm planning to make, and the other's for me. Across the bottom, he's written in black Sharpie:

For Diana, star of stage, screen, and Cinderella Cleaners. Yours, Adam

Wow, I think. *Even his handwriting's cute.*

I go online and print out some photos of scenes from the show. Then I put them and the signed 8 x 10 photo of Adam on a big piece of poster board left over from a science project. I measure the letters out carefully so it'll look really good. It takes a long time, but I'm proud of the way it comes out.

The next day is Friday. Jess and I go to the principal's office and ask her for permission to set up a table outside the cafeteria door, where sports teams and clubs hold bake sales. Ms. Wyant sets up a rotation of different drama club members to cover all lunches and after school. Jess and I sign up for the first shift, and Amelia and Sara sit with us in solidarity, even though they're not in the drama club.

"You sat with us at the soccer team bake sale," Amelia reminds me as Sara takes lids off today's takeout containers. Tandoori chicken, mango chutney, and jasmine rice. It smells wonderful. "Want some?" she says, and as always, we all chorus yes.

But before I eat even a bite, I set up the poster I made:

BUY ONE, GET TWO FREE!
YOUR *OUR TOWN* TICKET ENTERS YOU IN A RAFFLE FOR
TWO FRONT-ROW SEATS
TO SMASH HIT BROADWAY MUSICAL
ANGEL!

Right under the words is the 8 x 10 photo of Adam. It acts like a magnet.

"OMG, he was on *Gossip Girl*!"

"I heard that show's great!"

"Front-row tickets, for real?"

"He is mega-cute!" This last is from Kayleigh, who seems to be noticing that we exist again. Next to her, Ethan shoves his hands into his pockets, muttering, "He's not *that* cute." But even Ethan has to admit that we've found a great way to sell tickets. Flocks of girls stop by, all fluttery, and even a couple of boys dig into their wallets. Our math teacher, Mr. Perotta, buys six tickets. "Pick me a winner," he says as he hands Jess the money. Who knew he liked Broadway shows?

By the end of the day, we've sold most of the tickets for Friday night, and Saturday's filling up fast. But we don't stop there.

On Saturday morning, Jess and I bundle up in warm jackets and scarves and set up a card table outside the ShopRite where Will works on weekends. All day long, people stop to buy tickets — people who don't even have kids at Weehawken Middle School — and some of them even make extra donations to our drama club. When Will isn't rounding up carts from the parking lot, or unloading truckloads of produce, he comes and hangs out with us. He and Jess have become good friends during rehearsal, which takes the edge off his shyness.

"We're almost sold out!" Jess beams, shaking the cash box.

"Sweet." Will picks up the autographed program from *Angel* and flips through the pages. "I checked out the show's Web site last night. The music is totally cool. Usually rock music and Broadway don't really go, but these guys got it right."

From Will, this is practically a monologue. I'm impressed.

"You would love it," I say. "The bass player was awesome."

"Cool," says Will, drumming his fingers on top of the cash box. The rattling coins make it sound like a snare drum, and he thumps the edge of the table with his other hand, working up a real solo before he stops. Jess and I clap and whistle.

"My father's a drummer," he says, and then, "I should get back to work."

"Supervisor?" I ask, and he nods grimly.

"Watches the clock like a hawk."

"I've got one of those at the cleaners," I tell him. "They need to get a life."

"Really," says Will, getting up. "See you tonight, okay?" I watch him lope off toward the loading dock as Jess wags her fingers good-bye. I still think she's wrong about Will crushing on me, but I'm getting the sense he's a pretty nice guy once you get to know him.

That night I sit in the auditorium lobby with my *Angel* poster and a tall glass jar, collecting the ticket stubs as raffle tickets. "Be sure to write your name and phone number on the back," I tell people as they stream in. "We'll be doing the drawing right after the play."

Amelia and Sara are handing out programs. "We're almost sold out," Sara says. "Good thing we left coats on our seats."

They're sitting together in back, but Jess has saved two seats for me and her mother, fifth row on the aisle. When everyone else has gone in and the houselights start blinking, I carry my jar down the aisle to my seat, which is one of the few that's not taken. Our school auditorium isn't as glamorous as a Broadway theatre, and I'm wearing a sweater and leggings instead of a satin dress, but there's that same expectant buzz in the air. As I take my seat, I see Jess's mom craning her neck just like I did at *Angel*. The curtains are open, and just as the playwright had wanted, the stage is bare.

"Where's the scenery?" somebody's dad says behind us, and I smile to myself. I can picture the whole cast backstage. I can imagine who's doing their vocal warm-ups and stretches, who's horsing around in the band room, and who's bent over nervous, afraid they might puke.

"Break a lo mein," I mentally whisper to Jess, as the lights start to dim. Mrs. Munson sits forward. It's magic time.

Riley ambles out in the Stage Manager's trademark suspenders, leaning against the arch as he tells the audience what they're going to see on this day in Grover's Corners, New Hampshire, 1901. He seems completely relaxed as he strolls around the stage, describing the buildings on Main Street. A couple of stagehands roll out two vine-covered trellises, and he says, "There's some scenery for those who think they have to have scenery." The audience ripples with laughter.

The first act rambles on, some good and some bad. There are the usual missed lines and stiff-as-a-board kids in bit parts, but also some scenes that are great. Jess does a terrific job nagging her children to get ready for school, and I wonder if her mother's blushing. Kayleigh's kind of full of herself, but she knows what she's doing.

At the end of Act One, the stagehands push two ladders onto the stage so Emily and George can talk through the upstairs windows of their neighboring houses. And when Lillie Chu, the tiny sixth grader playing George's kid sister, tells him in her sweet, high-pitched voice about a letter addressed to Grover's Corners, New Hampshire, United States, all the way up to "the Earth, the Solar System, the Universe, the Mind of God . . . and the postman brought it just the same," I'm as thrilled as she is.

The second and third acts go by in a blur. When the lights come back up for the curtain call, the audience claps and whoops as if we've just seen the best play in history. I hear someone backstage yell out a "*Yeah!*" and the audience laughs and claps even harder. The cast starts applauding back.

Then Riley steps forward and signals the lights back down to halfway. "Time for our raffle," he says, beckoning me from the audience. I climb onto the stage with my jar full of ticket stubs, shaking it up. "Our door prize tonight is two front-row tickets for *Angel*," I say.

Riley flashes a grin. "May I have the envelope, please?"

How did he know this was one of my dreams? Beaming, I reach deep down into the jar and hand him a ticket stub, which he unfolds.

"And the winner is . . . Jessica Munson, with love from Mom!"

Jess screams louder than anyone else. She stumbles out of the curtain call line, excited and looking totally amazed. I'm as happy as she is. We scream, hug each other, and jump up and down. I remember what Nelson said to me once: Things don't have to be perfect to come out just right.

Over Jess's shoulder, I see Will in the wings with his headset on, clapping and grinning like everyone else. He flips a switch on the sound board and the whole auditorium's flooded with music: the theme song from *Angel*. Will stands there swaying in time to the beat, and it's not hard to picture him playing a bass guitar.

Hmm.

Maybe he *is* kind of cute.

Turn the page for a sneak peek at

Cinderella CLEANERS

#2: Prep Cool

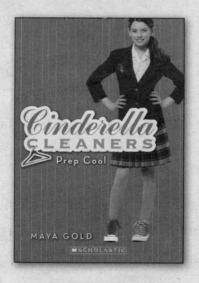

I've already told everyone I have stuff to do at the cleaners, and that Cat is picking me up after school. Sure enough, when we get out to the curb, the van is pulled up at the end of the long line of school buses.

I hop into the passenger seat next to Cat. "Hey, those braids are cute," she says as I buckle my seat belt. She starts up the van. "You got all your stuff?"

I'm already wearing the earrings and shoes, and I've stashed the rolled-up blazer and skirt in my backpack, along with the glasses and a map of the campus I printed last night. Yesterday, Cat hid the blouse, still in its cleaner bag, under a tarp in the back of the van. All I need now is a place I can change.

"Don't sweat it," says Cat. "This is a drivable dressing room. I'll pull over at one of those lookout points up on the cliffs." She turns on the radio, singing along like she always does.

Sure enough, a few miles out of town we come to a parking lot next to a heavy stone wall and a couple of coin-operated viewing machines that look like they've been there for ages. It's one of those clear but crisp days, when it's warm in the sunshine and cold in the shade, and the wind has the snap of a freshly picked apple.

I climb into the back of the van, crouch down, and peel off the sweater I'm wearing over my cami, swapping it for the white blouse. Then I pull on the plaid skirt, safety-pin its loose waistband, and wiggle out of my funky striped leggings. I unroll the blazer and pull it on, tugging the sleeves down as far as I can. I'm starting to get butterflies in my stomach, as if I'm backstage in the dressing room.

"How's it going back there?" Cat calls over the radio.

"Good." I make my way back to the front seat and fasten my seat belt. As Cat pulls away from the parking lot, I unbraid my hair. Just as I hoped, it's wavy and full. With the side part, it covers a lot of my face.

When we reach the next stoplight, I put on the tortoise-shell glasses and turn toward Cat. "What do you think?"

She glances my way. "You're a total Before picture."

"That was the plan. I'm going for stealth moves."

"Is that what you call it?"

We're driving along the cast-iron fence that surrounds the Foreman Academy. I'm reviewing my plan in my head. Get into the girls' dorm, figure out which room is Brooke's, find the phone. Of course, there's a chance it won't *be* in her room, that she's got it with her, in which case I'll have to step up to Plan B.

"The gatehouse is right up ahead, but you better drive past it to let me out. I don't want the security guard to see me getting out of the van."

Cat nods and drives past the gatehouse, slowing slightly to look down the driveway. She lets out a low whistle. "Whoa. This is some crib."

"I know, right?"

There's an ice cream stand just down the road. Cat pulls in and parks. "I bet all the preppies come in here to get slushies and stuff," she says as I open the door and climb out. "Unless they all drink Frappuccinos. What time do you want me to pick you up?"

"Quarter of three, I guess. Right before work."

She frowns. "It's not even noon yet."

"I'm not sure how long it'll take. But if I get out sooner, I'll wait inside. I'll be the one drinking a slushie."

"Okay," she says. "Be careful. I don't want to be posting your bail for impersonating a rich girl."

"I promise." Cat gives me a high five through the open window and drives away. I'm all by myself. I can feel my heart pounding, but can't really tell if I'm scared or excited. The ice cream stand has a big window, and I can see my reflection. I look pretty different from the girl who went to the Foreman dance Saturday night, but the question is, can I pass for Annika Reed? And there's only one way to find out.

I walk back along the fence until I reach the gatehouse. Leaning forward so my frizzy hair covers more of my face, I nod toward the guard at the window and walk quickly past.

"Hold on there," he says. "I need your pass."

Pass? Oh, no! I didn't think of *that*. I dig around in the blazer's right pocket, and then in the left. "I must have dropped it," I stammer.

"What time did you sign out?" The guard is a fatherly African-American man wearing thick glasses that are a lot like the ones I have on. I hope this will cause him to like me.

"Um, early?" *Before you came on duty, whenever that was.* I hope that he'll let me pass, but he takes out a clipboard with signatures.

"What's your name?"

"Annika Reed," I say, wincing and crossing my fingers.

"Reed?" he says, scanning the list with a frown.

I'm cooked. I won't even get onto the campus before I get kicked out. I stare at his clipboard list, trying to read upside down. "There was a UPS truck coming in at the same time. About nine in the morning?" I *hope* that's a nine I see next to his hand.

"Here it is — 9:05 A.M." He points. "Nick wrote down the truck coming in, but not you going out."

"Well, he gave me a pass," I say, trying to sound just impatient enough to move this along. "Is there some kind of problem? Just sign me back in."

I guess attitude does the trick, because he looks at me, sighs, and writes down ANNA K. REED and the time. "You hold on to your pass next time, hear?" I nod and he waves me through.

Now what?

My heart pounds extra loud as I walk down the long driveway onto the campus.

Read Them All!

Accidentally
Fabulous

Accidentally
Famous

Accidentally
Fooled

Accidentally
Friends

How to Be a Girly Girl
in Just Ten Days

Miss Popularity

Miss Popularity
Goes Camping

Making Waves

Life, Starring Me!

Juicy Gossip

Callie for President

Totally Crushed